Arabian Tales

ARABIAN TALES

Baghdad-on-Thames

KHALID KISHTAINY

QUARTET BOOKS

First published in 2011 by
Quartet Books Limited
A member of the Namara Group
27 Goodge Street
London W I T 2LD

A catalogue record for this book
is available from the British Library

ISBN   978 0 7043 7250 4

Typeset by Antony Gray
Printed and bound in Great Britain by
T J International Ltd, Padstow, Cornwall

Contents

A Handful of Rubbish   7

The Orange and the Ball   21

At the Government Expense   33

A Matter of Cats and Dogs   43

The Handkerchief   55

The Cost of Old Sins   69

For Love and Money   77

Fairuz   91

Talking of Organs   97

Dedication   109

Pioneers of the Cooperative Movement   111

Love per Hour   125

Write a paper and F**k the World   131

The Love of God and the Love of Man   137

Blessed are the Meek and the Innocent
    – the World in the Ears of a Child 141

Through a Hole:
    A Muslim–Christian Dialogue 145

Service to the Nation 149

What did Adam say to Eve? 163

A Woman in Metamorphosis 167

A Handful of Rubbish

Having done with the three days of formal speeches, debates, presentations, discussions and tedious listening to outdated papers and long repetitive poems, the Conference for Arab Solidarity, to which I was invited as a participant, came to its end with a long 'Call for Action' declaration. With a deep sigh of relief I returned to my hotel room. The time for the real work and discharge of responsibilities came at last. I opened my briefcase and took out the list of shopping for myself and my friends:

- Two bottles of Zahlawi Arak
- A box of baklawa pastries from al-Zuhur Confectioners
- One kilogram of zatar spice
- A copy of the *Perfumed Gardens Sex Manual*
- A handful of earth from Iraq for Abdul Maqsud.

Here, I stopped. A handful of earth from our homeland! Something to wonder about as the muezzin started to raise his voice from the distant minarets of old Baghdad, calling on all Muslim believers to hurry to their local mosques. It is very intriguing to notice

7

what Arab expatriates in Europe yearn for and miss in their dispersion. Uncle Haj Masud, aged seventy as he claimed or eighty as his wife, pot belly, Samira, put him, asked me once to bring him a circumcision master bag to remind him of the good days of his childhood and especially the day when he was circumcised together with his five brothers, all eventually killed in Saddam Hussein's wars. The *Perfumed Gardens Sex Manual* was requested by an older man, Sheikh Abd al-Gaffur, who found the Viagra pills useless and an utter waste of money. In a previous trip to Egypt I brought him a copy of the Arabic classic, The *Return of the Old to His Youth and the Rejuvenation of the Libido*. That was another disappointment for him. There was the Cultural Attaché who asked me to bring him his secondary school certificate to frame and hang in his office, for all to see that he was a graduate.

Just before leaving London, I managed to prepare that list of things which my friends and relatives wanted me to bring them from Iraq. A bottle of Arak for Dr Husni. Another one for Haj abdul Munim. A one kilogram box of kananfa cakes for Mrs Said. A box of almond stuffed dates, and so on. They were all very sensible and prudent requests, as soon there would be no Arak made in Lebanon, no kanafa cakes to be found in Damascus, no palm trees in Iraq to produce dates and conceivably no oil produced in Arabia or no Western customers to buy it from them.

But Abdul Maqsud's order for earth from his dusty homeland puzzled me. We became very close friends since our bloody punch-up over the Six Day War between the Arabs and Israel. He gave me a painful punch in the face as soon as I questioned his faith that Jamal Abd al-Nasser would, in a couple of days, be at the gates of Tel Aviv. It is always better in the Middle East to start with a good fight and then have peace and a lasting friendship than to start with a good friendship and end up with a lasting enmity.

'Dear Maqsud, I am going to Iraq in a few days. They invited me to the Conference for Arab Solidarity. Is there anything you want me to bring you on my way back? Anything you fancy or you are missing here in London? Please tell me. Don't feel embarrassed to ask.'

With a deep and tormented sigh, Abdul Maqsud looked at me with bewilderment and sorrow; 'No. There is nothing I want. There is nothing left there in our country worth buying and carrying. Thank you all the same, dear Khalid.'

Yet, knowing how nostalgic and yearning for anything from his old home, I persisted in my attempt to serve this old friend of mine. 'Surely there must be something you would like me to bring you; a basket of Barhi dates, some sweat pomegranates from Mandali or some traditional silverware. Come on, Maqsud, tell me.'

A few more seconds passed with his face becoming

grimmer and all the old lines sinking deeper and looking darker like those on a shrivelled dry lime. He opened his small eyes at last: 'Yah. I do want something. Bring me a handful of earth from Iraq. Just enough to fill a small glass jar to put on the mantel-shelf to look at and smell from time to time. When my hour comes, I want them to bury that handful of earth with me in this foreign land of the Christians. Make sure that you bring me a clean and pure piece of Mesopotamian soil from our homeland.'

'Ay! Some thing very cheap for a very dear friend.'

'No, Abu Niall, don't say so! The earth of our homeland is not cheap. It is mixed with the blood of millions of our brave ancestors over thousands of years, great men who stood and built great civilisations and defended them with their blood. We are the cheap ones. We are the ones who desecrated that land and sold it so cheap.'

Maqsud's words re-echoed in my mind as I was checking my shopping list. The departure hour was getting nearer and the delegates, news reporters and intelligence 'minders' crowded the hotel lobby, watching each other carefully all the time whilst discussing the latest news, i.e., the price of gold, the exchange rates and the temperature in Zurich. Suitcases, briefcases filled with cash bounties and wooden cases of various merchandise and gifts cluttered the corridors and the main entrance.

The simple handful of earth requested by my

friend suddenly acquired a supernatural proportion. 'A clean and pure piece of Mesopotamian soil from our homeland.' Where do I find that in this large city so polluted with broken sewers, mosquito-infested swamps and human refuse? Where do I find the soil of our homeland? Would it be in the gardens of this foreign Intercontinental Hotel, where the foreign tourists and oil entrepreneurs stretch on the deck chairs with their mistresses, stripped almost naked by the swimming pool and gazed at by the local rich businessmen and corrupt bureaucrats with their hungry eyes?

No, this is not our dear homeland. With that in mind, I left the Intercontinental with a plastic bag in hand to look for a pure piece of Mesopotamian soil, a handful of clean earth from our homeland for my friend Maqsud. I passed through a labyrinth of narrow lanes covered with broken bricks, pebbles of all sizes and colours, empty bottles and Coca Cola cans, rusty old bicycle wheels and piles of rotting food. In the midst of all this jumble ran streams of rotten water; you hear them and smell them but you don't see them, like the women around. Is this our homeland? Is this the place to carve up a handful of earth for my friend? No! Not here. I walked on to look for a clean piece of Mesopotamia.

With the plastic bag in hand bearing the legend 'Delicious Halal Food', I pursued my search along the entire Rashid Street, the main thoroughfare of

Old Baghdad, flanked on both sides by decaying buildings, mosques and shops, all with dusty walls and pillars bearing pictures and words such as 'Imperialism will be smashed by Arab Unity', 'Death to the traitors and Zionist agents', 'With our blood Palestine will live'. You can tell that you are in the old city not from any particular gates or historical buildings but from the smell of its decay and pissing corners, reserved for men only. I looked around. Is this our homeland where last night's vomit of the drunkards was still festering and mixing with the shit of the children and the droppings of the mules and asses. Is this the place where I can obtain a small amount of clean earth to take with me back to London? No. This is not our noble homeland. I walked on searching for it.

From Bab al-Muaddam, I took a boat and crossed the Tigris River and headed south. My footsteps led me finally to Sheikh Maruf Cemetery. All Arab towns are surrounded by the graves of the dead to remind you, lest you should forget, that those who died are more than those who lived and that the congestion you suffered on your way here is far less than the congestion you will encounter on the day of judgement. You enter any Arab town through a cemetery and leave it from another cemetery. Yes. That is a good place to pick up a handful of clean earth unadulterated by the sins and filth of the town. From earth to earth, from ashes to ashes. Out of this eternal bio-chemical recycling process, I may surely obtain a handful of worthy earth out of the remaining dust of worthy compatriots who gave their lives in the service of the nation.

> HE THE ONE WHO IS ETERNAL
> Here lies the remains of Samiha Amir,
> buried in the Prime of her youth
> with her babe buried in her womb.
> Shed a tear for them and
> pray the Almighty to forgive them.

I stopped and held tight the 'Delicious Halal Food' plastic bag which I had just filled with dust from the foot of her grave. Why had she died in the Prime of her youth? Was she killed to cleanse the family honour? Was it her lover who killed her, or more likely her husband? How had they killed her? With a kitchen knife, a single bullet, a rope around her neck? Maybe she wasn't killed at all. She died in labour or of puerperal fever. Pray that the Almighty may forgive her, or forgive her doctor, if there was one. What about the baby who was not even born? What sins did it commit to pray to God to forgive it? I looked at the small gravestone again and shuddered. No! This is no worthy handful of earth from our wretched homeland. I emptied my plastic bag and left the cemetery hurriedly to look yet again for our worthy homeland. But where?

It was almost high morning with very little time left

in hand. So, I pressed on in my search until I found myself outside the city in the midst of farms and palm tree orchards, still in a virginal state untouched by land speculators or army boots. Yes, that is our ancestral land, the land of the twin rivers, historical Mesopotamia. Surely I should be able to pick up a good handful of clean earth from this lush area, which I did indeed. But no sooner did I bend down to carve up some soil than a whole pack of hungry-looking dogs attacked me, barking and biting at my trousers and legs. 'Please, let go! Let go! I am no stranger. I am one of you. Believe me! A true Iraqi, a creature of this land. Don't bite me! Oh, don't . . . '

A bunch of men, peasants, appeared with old swords, daggers and sticks shouting and threatening: 'A thief! Dates thief! We'll show you, you fucking bugger . . . '

As they drew nearer, they calmed down and lowered their weapons and sticks. 'No. This is no dates thief. He is an effendi, a gentleman.' The headman shouted at the dogs, 'Stupid beasts! Can't you tell? This is no thief.'

'Dogs can't tell the difference between a gentleman and a thief,' said another as he went on kicking the dogs and lashing at them, sending them away howling and yelling.

'Sorry, sir. Forgive them. They are only dogs. They have no brain like us. They couldn't tell. You see, we are poor people and have only these palm trees to live on. Thieves from the Shariqi tribe are pestering us with their robberies, stealing dates from us,' said the headman as he started to examine my legs and attend to my wounds.

'Never mind! Never mind. I only wanted to take a little of your good earth,' said I as I showed them the little plastic bag filled with earth.

The men started to whisper among themselves. 'Don't you see? He is an engineer. An oil engineer.'

'They must be looking for oil in this area.'

'I heard it said. They say that there is oil here, at the Salhia.'

'God's mercy! To think that we'll have an oil well here in this farm! They can jolly well cut down these bloody palm trees and burn the wretched things.'

'Oh God! To think we'll be oil sheikhs and look straight in the face of those filthy emirs of the Gulf who treated us all these years like dirt on their shoes.'

With a sweeping gesture from his hand, the headman silenced all this hubbub and came forward towards me. 'Ustath, you are welcome here, any time you want to come. Take whatever earth samples you want for your work. With the blessings of God and his Messenger and Imam Ali, peace be upon them, you may succeed and find oil enough under this farm.'

With another gesture, he beckoned to the rest; 'Boys, Give our guest more earth.' Little boys in tattered dishdash rushed forward to refill my plastic bag with more dust. With that done, they started to fill my pockets as well with the same pale brown earth. There was no way for me to stop them. I just had to thank them for their generosity and wish them well. Far away from the impoverished farm and quite out of sight, I emptied my pockets and dusted my jacket and trousers, retaining only what was left in the bag inscribed 'Delicious Halal Food'.

Three innocent words. But anything innocent arouses the suspicion of security officers. 'Ustath, this doesn't look like food. What do you have in this plastic bag?' the security man at the Saddam Hussein International Airport asked me as he went on examining carefully my luggage, having already given up finding anything in the body search from the top of my head to the soles of my boots. ' "Delicious Halal Food", eh? What is that? Can I examine this bag?'

'Sure. No problem,' said I, offering him the bag before he asked me to give him my trousers, 'A mere handful of earth from your country.' I took a little amount of the dust and showed it to him in my hand. The officer, tall and broad, leaned over to smell it suspiciously with his big Semitic nose. 'Earth, you say? Or is it cocaine or some terrible drug to kill our people? Eh?'

He looked back and called on a colleague to come and smell the dust. The second officer invited a third one, a more senior officer, to join them in the smelling process. The three men held a war council

among themselves to set up the plan of action and the strategy for dealing with me. After repeated operations of smelling, testing and careful touching of the material in question, they reached the decision, with great disappointment on their faces, that this powder was not narcotic.

'But what is this dust? What do you want to do with it?'

'I have an old friend in London, someone from your country working with me. He feels very nostalgic for his homeland and asked me to bring him a handful of earth from Iraq to smell it and kiss it and keep it with him. He is very patriotic. He didn't leave his country during this regime, but during the defunct regime of many years ago.'

'What defunct regime are you referring to? We have had so many defunct regimes. Which of them?'

'Yes, true. You have had so many rotten defunct governments. I don't know which one of them he ran away from. But I think that my friend left your country a few years after the catastrophe, the nakba.'

'And which nakba you have in mind? We have had so many catastrophes in the recent years. Which of them?'

'Well, All I know is that he left the country between the defeat of 1948 and the set-back of the Six Days War of 1967.'

The senior officer looked at me with the same

suspicious expression to which all the muscles of his face had become tuned. But his lower lip protruded in this situation to convey the added expression of utter disdain for my person. 'A patriot, you say, wanting a handful of earth from his homeland?' said he contemptuously before turning to his colleague. 'You heard that Abu Haifa? A bunch of traitors and CIA agents boozing in London pubs and fucking English whores and they want a handful of earth from the homeland!' The man spat on the floor in front of me. In a sudden act of devotion to his duty and jealousy for his country, he hit my hand and caused all the earth to fall on the floor of the Departure Hall.

'A bunch of traitors and agents of imperialism,' said he indignantly, and pointed to the gate. 'Alright. Get on your plane.' He disdainfully put a cross on my suitcase and allowed me to pass. I closed it with the empty 'Delicious Halal Food' plastic bag and carried it through silently.

'Husni boy!' I heard him shouting as I left the checkpoint, 'Bring your broom and come and sweep this handful of rubbish!'

The Orange and the Ball

It was customary for the PE teacher in all the schools of Iraq to distribute oranges to the football players during half-time in any match against another school within the primary or secondary schools tournaments, with the notion that oranges contain enough vitamins and nourishment to guarantee the team victory over their opponents, who also happen to believe in the same idea and rely on oranges in their effort to win the trophy. Oranges, they argued, compensate the players for lost energy and turn every player into a Tarzan in the second half. In a hot and dry country like Iraq, the least any PE teacher worth his salt should see to is that something is consumed to replace the lost fluid as the players sweated it out on the pitch.

This long-standing custom observed by all competing schools was followed by the Askari Primary School which overlooked the old Tigris River, close to the Sarrafiah encampment with its miserable hovels and mud huts on the one side, and on the other side the lofty palaces and lush gardens of the prosperous middle class. The students, therefore, were a mixture of these two classes. Hamid happened to belong to the less fortunate lot. He lived with his two sisters and one younger brother, a mere toddler, in one of those depressing mud huts covered by straw planks, serving as bed-sitting-room and kitchen, all looked after by their mother, Um Hamid, a young widow who lost her husband in one of the countless battles fought against the Kurds in the north of the country. She earned their daily sustenance, bread and onions, by going out early in the morning to collect cows' dung for fuel and to sell to other slightly more fortunate peasant families.

Um Hamid couldn't afford any toys or games for her kids, not even a small rubber ball to play with. The two boys and their two sisters had to be content with improvised balls made out of old rags and news-papers, tied together with pieces of string, giving them a shape remotely resembling that of a ball. The four children went out of their hovel to play football in the street well into the night. When it was Hamid's turn to go to school, his dream was to join the school team and play with a real ball made of rubber and leather and filled with air – a ball that would bounce like the devil himself and not lie flat on its face as their rag ball did.

Having lost her husband in the civil war, early in her married life, Um Hamid turned all her attention to her little children. As soon as Hamid reached the age of seven, she washed him, dressed him as best as

she could and took him to al-Askary Primary School. There, she insisted on seeing the PE teacher, Mr Jasim Muhammad.

'This is my little fledgling, Hamid. We call him Hammudi. He lives and dies for football. He has no father. His dad was killed by the wicked Kurds in the mountains of Kurdistan in the north. We have never got his corpse back. You, sir, look like a good-hearted man who loves God and his Prophet. Please, look after my little boy. Treat him like your own son and God will reward you for it.'

The young widow bowed to kiss the teacher's hand but he withdrew it from her, fearing that he might catch something from her. But he promised the young widow to do everything he could for the hapless boy.

Hamid looked like a fragile young boy, with a pale face and thin limbs, always shy in dealing with his classmates. Yet his slender physique gave him some superiority over the other players in his speed and stamina. The long days which he spent playing football in the street with his rag ball, ever dribbling between the parked vehicles, passing traffic and pedestrians on the pavement, enhanced his skills in dealing with the proper ball on a proper football pitch covered with grass.

He was barely twelve, a pupil in the fourth form, when Mr Muhammad selected him for the school team and gave him the position of right winger. With his small body and superior speed, he outpaced and outmanoeuvred all his opponents to the delight of his teacher and classmates.

The first official match of the new season started with an encounter against the Kariat Primary School on the scouts' playing field. All players took their allotted positions, looking forward to the oranges which the PE teacher would dole out to them after the first half. They prayed to the Almighty Allah to make the oranges a well-deserved reward for a successful performance with one or two goals scored in their favour in front of their young supporters and headmaster. One of them recited the Kursi verse from the Qur'an. He was told the Kursi verse would ensure success for any sincere believer, even in helping him to score goals in a football match. Another boy preferred to recite the brief sura of 'Say thou that Allah is one,' which he repeated to himself no less than a dozen times. With his back to the young spectators, Husni turned his face northward towards, as he mistakenly thought, the holy city of Karbala, with its twin golden shrines of Imam al-Abbas and Imam al-Hussein. 'Please, hot-headed Imam Abbas,' he muttered to himself, 'make the goalkeeper of the Kariat School blind and let me score against him. Give us victory against these Kariat bastards. Don't let us go back disappointed.' Undoubtedly the Kariat players made a similar appeal to the good Imam, which must have caused him some bewilderment as to whom he should give his support and whose goal-keeper he should make blind.

The referee looked at his watch and whistled for the start of the match. Like elves in white shorts, the little players burst out running in every direction, shouting instructions, swearing and chasing the ball from right to left and from left to right aimlessly. Their fellow pupils were bouncing, yelling and waving their arms on the terraces, urging them, encouraging them and chanting, 'Marching on, marching on all the way, marching on.' For them it looked like a battle on which the whole of Iraq or indeed the whole Middle East depended. They waved their banners, flags and sticks and even their shirts, 'Marching on to the cup, all the way to the cup!'

The noise went on unabated until the referee whistled for half time. The young supporters rushed on to the field to embrace their favourite players, each encouraging his home team. Jasim Muhammad, the PE teacher, led the way with the school porter, Abu Abdulla, carrying the customary basket of oranges, eleven in all. Mr Muhammad took the basket and started the distribution, calling each player by his name, thanking and congratulating them on their performance. 'Said Wali – your orange. Abbas Kurdi – take this one. Hamdi Isa – come and get yours. Fadhil Ali – this one for you. Hamid Hussein. Oh, Hamid. Come here! Where are you? Don't be shy.'

Little Hamid came forward and was immediately embraced by his teacher who could not resist kissing him on the head and ruffling his short, thick hair, black like the pupils of his eyes. 'Well done, sonny. Well done. All credit to you!' He was the little boy who scored the only goal in the tournament against the Kariat Primary School. 'There – take this one.' The PE teacher picked the largest and best orange in the basket. 'Well you deserve it!' The shy and deprived child bashfully took the good orange, a true Baquba orange, the best and juiciest in the country.

The boys started to peel the oranges with their nails, munching with enjoyment, spitting out the large pips and throwing the pieces of peel onto the football pitch. They wiped their mouths on their new blue-and-white striped shirts and began to discuss the second half of the match. 'You, George, watch that son of a bitch, Sulayman, their right winger,' said the young captain. 'Don't ever let him out of your sight. Chase him wherever he goes. Kick him and put him out of play when you can. The bastard! He is a handful.'

The orders, advice and encouragement sounded between the players and between them and their teacher until the last moment when they heard the referee's whistle – the signal to start the second half, with the Askari School team having the advantage. Alas, the captain's advice was not properly observed as it should have been, for that 'son of a bitch', the right winger, Sulayman, managed to steal away from George, dribble through the defence and score the equalising goal. The match now turned into a pitched battle between these twenty-two players for the winning goal.

Their little faces were sweating and they were staggering on their tired legs and rather heavy boots, too heavy for their slender limbs. They were trembling and falling on each other like a bunch of black-winged ants. Hamid, so used to playing bare-foot in the street and around his mother's mud hut, stopped and took off his heavy leather boots and threw them out of the field. Mr Qadir, the part-time referee, watched him as he did so and winked at him as if to say, 'Alright little chap. I'll allow that for you.' The small crowd on the terraces went on chanting more vociferously, trying to raise the spirit of their players, 'Marching on, marching on, all the way, the Askari boys marching on.' The chant inter-mingled with the voices of the opponents: 'Kariat, first and last! First and last!'

There were only two or three minutes left to the final whistle when the tall goalkeeper of the Askari School made a spectacular save, held the ball firmly to his chest and then passed it on to the left-side defender, Abbas Kurdi, in a desperate attempt to start yet another counter-attack. Abbas flicked it on to little Hamid on the opposite side, who received it thankfully and handled it skilfully. He swerved right and then left, dribbling and out-pacing the Kariat defence, leaving one on the floor and the other standing helplessly, until there was nobody between him and the goal other than the goalkeeper himself. The field was wide open for him to hit the back of the net and settle the match in favour of the Askari team. The tumult of the Askari supporters was deafening, urging and encouraging, 'Come on, Hamid! Go on Hamid! This is your goal.' There were no more than four or five metres between him and the goal when a large orange fell from the pocket of his shorts. He stopped abruptly, turned his back on the almost open goal, retracted his steps quickly towards the fallen orange, picked it up and put it back in his pocket. He did all that in seconds, but the ball had already drifted away from him safely towards the welcoming hands of Marzuq, the Kariat goalkeeper, who picked it up like a welcomed present and kicked it away as high as he could. The ball was still rising in the air when the referee looked at his watch, put the whistle in his mouth and blew the long note ending the inconclusive match.

The boys of the Askari Primary School, with their schoolmaster, Jasim Muhammad, to the fore rushed towards Hamid, swearing, screaming and gesturing with their hands. 'You little fool! You stupid wimp! Whatever happened to you? Have you lost your senses? You have an open goal in front of you and you stop to pick up an orange?'

Mr Jasim Muhammad took Hamid Hussein by the arm angrily, shaking and pushing him. 'Why do you still have this orange? Why didn't you eat it in the interval like the rest of your mates? Why are you hiding it in your pocket, eh?' he shouted at the confused and tearful boy.

'I want to take it to Mum, sir.'

'To Mum, you silly boy?'

'I want to eat it with Mum. I want Mum to taste an orange, sir.'

At the Government Expense

Whether trying in Britain to seduce your neighbour's wife or secure an overdraft from your bank manager, you start the conversation with the unfailing subject of the weather. In Iraq, the subject is always water, the water level of the twin rivers, the Tigris and the Euphrates. Since the neighbouring countries, Syria, Turkey and Iran, started diverting great quantities of the precious water to their massive reservoirs and ambitious agricultural projects, you hear them now-adays talking about how low the water level has gone down. 'Do you think we need a boat today to cross the river or shall we walk it?' But in *ayyam al khair,* the good old days, the subject was usually how high had the river risen since the morning or since last night. The question was very pertinent and serious in spring time when the two rivers and their tributaries start to rise and threaten to flood and, indeed, drown the capital, Baghdad, and most other southern cities.

But there is a second subject for a civilised con-versation, that is, the dates which used to be the main

export commodity for the country before oil was discovered. The citizenry were divided as is usual in Iraq.
There were those who believed that God sends the
summer heat, reaching sometimes more than 50°
Centigrade in the shade, to ripen the dates. Others
thought that it is the dates which cause all that
terrible heat in the month of August. I haven't yet
heard that the two parties fought it out in mighty
street battles over the subject. No one was slain and
no corpses were dragged into the city's public squares.

Thus it was in 1938 when the water level com-
manded very exceptional and ominous attention.
Everybody agreed that the Tigris River had never
reached such a threatening swell, almost audible. It
was all God's vengeance. What do you expect when
even Muslims start to sell arak outside the mosques?
Believers of all denominations went to their temples
to ask for God's forgiveness and mercy upon
their houses, properties and merchandise. But the
Almighty dismissed all their prayers and blew into
the murky brown water loaded with timber, broken
pieces of furniture, bird cages, tree trunks and empty
cans and beer bottles. With such anger and venom,
they knocked and smashed at the flimsy earthen dams
and barriers until the whole might of the old river
broke the back of the Nazim Pasha embankment
and raced rumbling into the streets of the precious
Waziria District, preparing and gathering force for
the final onslaught on the whole city of Baghdad.

All that when the city was fast asleep, except for a few police officers watching the river when it broke loose like a runaway prisoner and rushed away in every direction, rumbling and thundering. Telephones rang from one police station to another.

'Captain Adnan, wake up. Get a few lorries and fill them with compulsory volunteers to block the flow of the water immediately. A state of emergency will be declared.'

'Sir, where can I find any volunteers at this hour?' answered the police officer in charge of al-Sarai police station, Captain Adnan Muhiddin. 'Sir, it is past midnight and everybody has gone to bed. The streets and cafés are all empty. The mosques are shut and the dawn prayers won't begin before four in the morning'

'I don't care. Get them all out of their beds. They will all drown and die if they don't. The king will be furious. Do you want the city of Harun al-Rashid to be destroyed?'

With these words of frenzy, the Governor of Baghdad, General Nuri al-Qadisi, rang off and went back to sleep with his Hungarian mistress, leaving Captain Muhiddin in the lurch. He picked up the phone and rang Um Wasila, his wife. 'Darling, don't wait for me. I won't be able to come home tonight. Some very urgent business cropped up. Baghdad is in danger of flooding.'

'What else? Now it is the flood! What next? Why

don't you admit it like an honest man and say you fancied another fat-bottomed whore in Kallachia and you want to spend the night with her?'

The Kallachia! Ay! Ay! The great red light district of Baghdad. That is the place, Captain Muhiddin thought immediately. This is the only place which does not sleep at night in our country. No, rather it comes back to life at that time of the day. Scores of young, able-bodied men, working people and high-ranking professionals would be jostling and chasing after scores of tarted-up young females ready for hire; Kurds with grey eyes, Persians with rosy cheeks and runaway Arab pregnant peasants from the southern marshes with tattooed chins and cheeks.

Captain Muhiddin wasted no time in ordering his men, some thirty of them with their truncheons and guns, to drive the three available armed lorries to the Kallachia brothel land of the city and round up whatever men and women they found there: pimps, prostitutes, customers, barmen, restaurateurs and all.

It was not a very difficult task for the police force. The old mediaeval district of the approved sinful factory, stretching back to the days of the Mongol conqueror, Hulagu, in the thirteenth century, was a small labyrinth of narrow lanes winding through a score of ramshackle houses. They called it Kallachia (the place of heads) as it was the place where the Mogul officers used to count the heads of the slain

Muslims, Christians and Jews and pay the soldiers according to the number of heads brought thither. Over the years, the Baghdadis shunned the macabre area and left it to the sex workers and traders to populate and carry out their work.

Quite familiar with every nook and cranny of the district, Captain Muhiddin led the invasion and filled up his lorries with the willing and unwilling, dressed and undressed, men and women, some kicking and protesting as they were plucked away from the bosoms of their whores.

'Come along! Your country needs you,' shouted the young officer.

'I want my money back,' protested one client, a young sherbet seller. 'I haven't finished. I want my money back.'

'Come along, damn you! Is this the time to fuss about it?'

'Pull up your pants, man, and follow us!' added Sergeant Abdul Ghaffar, sternly.

At the edge of the Waziria district, to the north of Baghdad, they were given axes, spades and bundles of sacks. The men dug from the cemetery nearby, and filled the sacks with earth and the women carried them on their backs and on their heads to dump and fill the broken gap of the embankment. With thankful enthusiasm and vigour, the women ran forward and backward, singing, chanting and laughing loudly.

'What is the matter with you, Hamida? Why are you lagging behind?' Captain Muhiddin shouted.

'Just let me take off my shoes, officer. I am an Arab woman. We do things better when bare-footed.'

She managed, in the end, to get rid of the cumbersome high heels, threw them aside and picked up two heavy sacks full of earth, flung them onto her shoulders and ran with them like a young gazelle.

By the time the izzan from the minaret of the Adhamia mosque, 'Allahu Akbar! Allahu Akbar!' was heard, calling on all Muslims to hurry for the nearby masjid for the dawn prayers, the women had managed to close the gap and stop any more water rushing into the town. They sat and stretched on the ground, exhausted and breathless.

Back in their Kallachia, Captain Muhiddin addressed them with these words: 'Ladies and gentlemen, I have just spoken over the telephone with His Excellency the Governor of Baghdad and told him of your good work. His Excellency is most impressed by your achievement and patriotism and told me that in recognition of what you have done, all the men standing here before me are entitled to fuck any of the women they choose at Government expense. You, the good procurers and madams, please submit your bills directly to me to have them settled immediately. God bless you all.'

By the end of the fiscal year, the budget of the Governorate of the Metropolis of Baghdad included this item: '80 Dinars expense of sex provision pertaining to flood defences being 550 Fils per intercourse with condom and 500 Fils without.'

A Matter of Cats and Dogs

Habits in man and animal die hard. This obvious statement of an obvious fact may sound tedious, but consider the astonishing political consequences which often flow from such banalities, as in this present case. One of such habitual traits carried over by the Israelis from their former mediaeval life in Europe to their new home in the Middle East was their horror of dogs. There is a long tradition behind that horror, going back to the days when a good Christian used to express his religious fervour by setting the local dogs upon the wandering Jew passing along the highways and byways of Christendom. The dogs, who were not allowed to take part in the newly evolved sport of tennis and football, because of the prejudice of the commoners who were glad to find in the dogs a class lower than themselves, enjoyed the sport of mauling the Jewish traveller, scattering his merchandise and tearing up his long gabardine coat. The dogs were also gratified to find somebody lower than themselves in the ordered life of the period and enjoyed this exercise in Anti-Semitism.

Jewish fear of this canine animal became a logical

sequence which continued in the new Jewish state of
Israel. Its logic, however, began to strike a discordant
note in Israel and other immigrant countries with
the reality of the new life. On a cold day in November
1968, the day of the Karama battle – a skirmish
unknown to any military historian but a byword on
the lips of all Arab school children, of whom a considerable proportion of both sexes have now grown
up under the unhappy strain of bearing the simple
name of 'Karama' – added another element to the
national confusion of their country's registration
offices.

On the morning of that early winter's day, a unit
of the Israeli Army crossed the River Jordan and
occupied Karama, a little village perched on the hills
to the east of the historic river. In less than two
hours they had demolished all the houses, uprooted
scores of old olive trees, killed a few score of
Palestinian Arabs and confiscated the Parker ball
pen of the United Nations observer. Seeing that the
soldiers had begun to idle and lose morale, the commander of the attack force ordered a withdrawal and
sent his sergeant-major to inspect the improvised
little bridge.

'Sir,' the soldier reported back, 'the tanks can
cross; the armoured vehicles can cross. The heavy
guns can cross; the infantry cannot.' The commander
was stupefied as all commanders in the face of
any unmilitary logic. The sergeant-major went on to

explain: 'Sir, there is a fucking dog lying next to the cypress tree this side of the fucking bridge. We don't know where it came from.'

Amman Radio interrupted its martial music to give this news flash: 'Our valiant forces have encircled the enemy and cut their rear lines.' For once an Arab military communiqué bore some semblance of reality. The Israeli commander showered his headquarters with urgent cables, and waves of Mirages went swooping down with bombs, napalm and rockets at the lonely cypress tree. After the dog had been seen, through the binoculars, going up in smoke, the infantry made a safe crossing.

Such was the true and only objective account of the Karama battle as was given by word of mouth to Miss Judy N. Penchforth by the United Nations observer who lost his Parker pen and could not draft another UN report. Miss Penchforth was an old lady whose sympathies with the Arab cause went back to the days when she saw Colonel Lawrence riding a camel. As soon as Major Seymour O'Grady, the UN observer, came in his story to the part of the dog and its tragic death, Miss Penchforth fainted. When she came round, she was heard murmuring, 'Hitler was right! Hitler was right!' After a glass of brandy, she walked out of the United Nations office, got hold of an Arab refugee boy limping on a crutch and started to tell him how the wicked Jews killed the innocent dog.

Miss Penchforth rushed from one government department to another in Amman repeating to everybody that tragic tale. The Arabs were stunned. Why had they been wasting their time these past twenty years talking about the suffering of the Palestinian refugees when they could have done better by talking about the plight of the innocent dogs in the Holy Land? Everybody turned against the Jordanian Information Department. The head of that office, who did not happen to be related to the king, was fired for inefficiency and waste of public money. The left-wing press accused him of being CIA agent and swore that they were in possession of irrefutable documents supporting the claim.

A more sophisticated campaign was then planned on the basis of the dogs' plight under the Zionist rule. The campaign was supported with impressive data and statistics on the Dogs' Exodus of 1948, following the foundation of the Zionist entity, the decline of the dog population in Israel and the reduction of their status to a persecuted minority in the animal kingdom, with even the frogs and toads ahead of them. Pictures of starving Saluki dogs, the pride and joy of the nomadic Bedouins, were sent to all political organisations in Europe and America. This was followed by an appeal to the United Nations for an investigation into the story of the ten thousand graves dug up near Tel Aviv on the eve of the June War. It was claimed that the graves were meant and were actually used for a mass burial of living dogs. In the Negev, the Demona Nuclear Centre was presented as no more than a camouflaged extermination camp with gas chambers for the hated dogs. Experts in the Arab Bureau for the Boycott of Israel went so far as to spread the rumour that Israeli toys were made from dogs' fur, and that all Jaffa oranges were fertilised with dogs' bonemeal.

All this was contrasted with the position of dogs in the Arab countries where they were treated exactly as the majority of the human population and where, the propagandists went on to assert with the facts on their side, you could hardly point your finger at any distinction between the average human life of an Arab and a dog's canine life. In London, an exhibition was arranged in the crypt of St Martin-in-the-Fields with an Arab dog wearing a collar of barbed wire. In front of him was placed his daily United Nations ration – a small two-inch square biscuit. The legend on top read: 'Not by biscuit alone does a dog live. Help the animals of the Holy Land!'

This particular exhibition aroused the anger and disgust of the British public with their notorious weakness for animals. Thousands of men and women sent their dinner jackets and evening dresses in aid of the refugee dogs, and it was impossible to explain to the donors that dogs don't wear them. Eventually, they were sold in auctions and jumble sales organised by the Council for Justice to Animals, and tons of

Pal dogfood cans were bought and sent by air to Beirut and Amman. The greedy Arab refugees ate them all and only gave them to the dogs when somebody told them that they contained pork. Now only dogs and Christian refugees eat the Pal meat.

The Arab publicists felt more than gratified all round. At last the Israeli image was really tarnished and gloom descended on Tel Aviv. Massive funds and materials started to pour into the Arab capitals from all corners of the Western world. But God is equitable in his distribution. Now it was an American tourist, a Mrs Pointen, widow of a rich nylon manufacturer from Detroit, who listened to the same tale of the unfortunate Karama dog and the terror meted out by the Israelis to Arabs and dogs alike. But Mrs Pointen was not moved in the least. After a pause, she turned and asked with some apparent anxiety: 'And the cats too? What about the cats?' Mrs Pointen happened to be a cat lover.

The intelligence agents of Israel heard the story and, realising its utmost significance, wasted no time in communicating the report to their employers. Levy Eshkol, the Prime Minister of the Jewish State, called for a cabinet meeting immediately. A statement was carefully hammered out and delivered to the international bunch of journalists: 'Although many dogs have left the country of their own free will, the cats have remained in Israel and their number has even increased. They and the citizens of

Israel are getting on famously.' Together with the official statement, Davar carried a long editorial with a photograph showing a young kibbutznik teaching a Siamese cat to swim in the Sea of Galilee.

The Arab propagandists countered without difficulty. 'Ah!' they said, 'But cats are unfaithful creatures and their allegiance is not to man but to place.' They challenged Tel Aviv to give any figures on the increased number or the wellbeing of cats.

The Jewish Agency despatched its emissaries to the four corners of the diaspora with the precise slogan: 'Bring in the cats!'

The veteran David Ben Gurion lamented in his Negev retreat the lack of fulfilment of this decade of his life. He was let down. How could cats lead a truly cattish life outside the state of Israel? In London, the *Jewish Chronicle* commented that if only every Jewish family in Britain contributed just with one kitten to Eretz Israel, the young state could solve all its economic problems and become a truly viable entity. With his long experience in the aliya and resettlement of Jewish youth during World War II, the philanthropist, Mr Norman Bentwich, started his cat aliya.

But the leader and President of the United Arab Republic of Egypt, Jamal Abdul Nasir, was not sleeping all this time. From his Muntazah Palace in Alexandria, he could hear the loud mewing disturbing the silence of the sea as the noise went up from the loaded ships steaming through the Mediterranean en route to Jaffa. At 3.30am on a cold February night, the Soviet Ambassador was awakened from his sleep. The Egyptian President wanted him on the telephone. Moscow must honour its commitments! The balance of forces was seriously disturbed. Within three days, the Illushin transport aeroplanes went into action ferrying to Egypt heavy loads of Moscovite terriers, Volga boat bitches, Eskimo huskies and Azbikistani sheep dogs. The American military experts who followed the operation closely admitted that Soviet military efficiency left nothing to be desired in that historical February dogs' airlift. If the Soviets could carry out the deployment of dogs with such ease, what would they do with mere human beings in time of war?

The Egyptians, on the other hand, showed everything that stood in contrast to the Soviet military efficiency. The customs police, seeing that the dogs carried no foreign currency with them, simply let them pass without further ceremony. The free dogs, now counted in thousands, marched straight to the great Mosque of Abu al-Abbas under the guidance of the sheep dogs from Muslim Azbikistan. There they were met by the usual crowd of native dogs waiting for alms, and a bloody battle ensued immediately. The sermon of the Friday preacher was drowned by the barking of the animals and no one could hear a syllable of the Qur'an. So the preacher left his pulpit and ran up the winding spiral stairs to address the dogs from the top of the Minaret. With both arms stretched out, he shouted to the dogs, 'You are all brothers.' But his words achieved no better results than those spoken from the pulpit. The Russian dogs knew no Arabic to understand him, and the Egyptian dogs had already heard too much talking of brotherhood. The police were eventually called in and the native and foreign dogs were only separated after some blood letting and machine-gun crackling. The scene of the battle featured in nearly every newspaper in the western world and brought in the high dividends dreamed of by President Nasir. 'Help the Egyptian dogs' societies were formed in most American towns and even the Zionist congressional lobby had to keep a low profile, in deference to American public opinion, when President Johnson submitted an emergency financial bill in aid of the Middle East dogs.

In the meantime, the fight for more dogs and more cats on both sides of the cease-fire line continued unabated. The Israeli propagandists, always one up on the Arabs, introduced a talking cat on Tel Aviv Radio. Dov, the cat, was trained to pronounce the two syllables of 'me . . . rvy', a cattish abbreviation for 'marvellous'. To every question put by the Kol-Israel interviewer, Dov, the cat, answered 'Me . . . rvy'. How did you find life in the Jewish state? 'Me . . . rvy.' How are the cats treated by the people of Israel?

'Me . . . rvy.' How did you find your holiday in the Kibbutz? 'Me . . . rvy.' And so on. Millions of people in New York listened to the ten-minute programme, 'With Dov, the Cat' broadcast by Kol Israel every evening. Shiploads of double-chinned American millionaires with fat wives and fatter wallets went on pilgrimage to Israel, the fat-cat country.

The Arabs soon caught on and started to hit back in a panoramic manner. Hundreds of dogs were led into the studios of Cairo Radio to bark and whine at the microphone for hours on end. The radio station of Baghdad which used to beam a nightingale serenade from its transmitters as its distinctive station signal, now replaced that by a dog barking. The poor Bedouins of the Syrian desert, always travelling with Japanese transistor radios tied to the necks of their camels, took note that the lingo of the townspeople was getting wilder and wilder. 'Easy, easy, you son of a dog,' they shouted at the radio. England, duty bound not to supply strategic materials to the Middle East, contented herself by sending tins of Kit-E-Kat to Israel and Pal dog-meat, with real liver, to Jordan.

The Israeli government highly praised the nourishing values of the Kit-E-Kat tins, issued them with Kosher certificates and gave them to their oriental Jews to eat. The Jordanian refugees, still swearing that there was pork in Pal tins, traded them for humus with the Lebanese Maronites who then made a profit on them by selling them back to England. A certain Hanna al-Khuri, a merchant from Sidon, who made his fortune by selling Sainsbury's tinned whole lamb hearts to sick peasants as potential spare parts for heart transplants, set up a new company in Cyprus to deal with the new Middle East line of business.

The affair reached sickly proportions and *The Times* of London could not but carry a fully-fledged editorial on this futile conflict between Jew and Arab. Urging the four powers to put an end to the costly race, the Middle East editor of the newspaper aptly remarked that the fight for more cats and more dogs by the two sides had really become a rat race.

The following morning the editor received an urgent cable from the same astute merchant of Sidon, Mr Hanna al-Khuri, with these words: 'Please advise – where are the rats?'

The Handkerchief

It is most understandable for any woman, of good and ill breeding alike, to refuse to listen to any explanation from her husband for the shocking discovery of a lady's perfumed handkerchief in his underpants whilst taking off his trousers in front of her and her children. 'Don't "dear" me!' repeated Mrs Harrington every time her husband tried to open his mouth with 'Listen, my dear . . . '

'You should be ashamed of yourself. At your age, the managing director of Royal Deodorants Consolidation, mixing with Middle East whores! Look at this,' she said to her city gentleman of a husband, pointing to the Arabic inscription on the handkerchief. 'A dirty Arab prostitute! A busy committee meeting with a prostitute every Thursday evening!'

'But listen, my dear. I really don't know whether she was Arab or Persian, what . . . '

'No, you don't know,' she interrupted him for the tenth time, 'You don't even know where she comes from. You don't care! Anything in a skirt will do for you.'

Just when the respectable Mr Harrington was

about to resume his unfinished sentence, there was another outburst from his wife: 'Christ! Who is this grinning, blood-curdling vampire? Who is he? Homosexuality – I've always suspected it. My God!' The unsuspecting woman thrust the lace handkerchief into Mr Harrington's hands revealing the printed picture on its corner, and started to sob.

Little did any of them know the full story of this little piece of white material on its long hazardous journey across mountains and seas on its way to Mr Harrington's underpants, or the part which it had played in the rich history of Babylon in earlier days when children used to play and not simply sit around and watch the grown-ups play, when men were men and shaved their pubic hair and not their beards and moustaches, and when tailors fixed buttons to men's trousers instead of the erratic fly zippers. That was a time when the Sole Leader was first released from his sealed bottle with the magic formula of 'Hey! Coup d'état!', three times repeated by three senior officers of a tanks brigade at the first crow of a cock, and proceeded to fill the earth and skies of Babylon with his portraits. Anything prohibited became instantly permitted merely by the judicious addition of the Leader's portrait; anything barred from importing into the land was allowed as long as it carried the picture of the Leader. Bubble gum for the kids, false teeth for the old, American stockings for the women, steel crutches for the cripples were all given import licences free from all customs' duties as long as they carried the portrait of the Leader printed on them with a suitable caption of praise and adoration.

This gentle device of getting around the law saved many business houses from the destruction of the protection decrees. Ali Chalabi, an importer of foreign garments and fine lingerie, had his application for Hong Kong-made socks granted in full just by incorporating the Leader's image into the pattern of the socks. When the Leader examined his application, he scribbled in the margin the question: 'Where will he put my picture?' Ali Chalabi simply replied to the sole Leader, 'Of course on the sole.' And the Sole Leader put his signature, 'To be granted.' The purchase of these socks was then made compulsory throughout the armed forces, prisons, orphanages and mental asylums.

Inspired by such an encouraging appreciation from the government, Ali Chalabi went on to import ladies' handkerchiefs and men's silk ties with the same decorative motive. Mrs Hana al-Wasily, the President of the Revolutionary Women's Federation, announced that no woman would be admitted to the membership of the Revolutionary Federation without buying at least one lace handkerchief from Mr Chalabi's merchandise. As no woman in Iraq could find any employment without the Revolutionary Federation's card, the announcement amounted to an order that no woman should be given any job without carrying Mr Chalabi's handkerchief.

'How dare you!' shouted Mrs Hana al-Wasily at her secretary one day as she sneezed all over her desk and her new fur. 'How dare you produce in my presence an ordinary miserable hanky? Where is your Leader's handkerchief?' The poor girl panicked, stammered and could only say with a broken voice, 'But . . . but do you want me to spit at his image every time I cough?'

Mrs Wasily found the question really perplexing and could only point to the door and dismiss the unhappy secretary without answering her question. After ten minutes of painful thought, she reached the conclusion that this was going to be another bad day and, succumbing to this realisation, she opened her handbag and took two Valium tablets.

However, on further consultations and committee deliberations, it was resolved that every member of the Revolutionary Woman's Federation should carry two handkerchiefs, one with the picture of the Leader as a sign of love and devotion, and one plain for the purpose of spitting. It was also resolved that Mr Ali Chalabi should be given another licence to import a second consignment of plain handkerchiefs.

Upon hearing of this new revolutionary measure, the Sole Leader invited Mrs Wasily and all serving members of the Executive Committee of the Revolutionary Women's Federation, together with the young secretary who sneezed, Miss Poran Said. They were met by all the top brass of the armed forces in an extended reception in which the Leader delivered another long speech on the imperialist conspiracies hatched against the Republic and the vigilance of the people exemplified by young Poran Said in her intelligent stance. A young officer with the rank of captain then stepped forward and presented Miss Said with a small box, but elaborately decorated, containing a lace handkerchief embroidered in real gold with the portrait of the Leader. With tears in her eyes, Miss Said lifted the handkerchief carefully like a precious piece of old papyrus and exhibited it to her colleagues, upon which everybody, including the Leader, breathed, 'Ah!' The whole occasion was then televised and recorded for posterity.

'This is the most precious thing a woman can have in all her life,' said Mrs Wasily to her young secretary. 'The Leader's handkerchief, presented by the Leader himself. You must be very careful with it. The agents of imperialism will simply mug you and rob you of it.' But Poran was not short of advisers on this point as everybody tried to become an old uncle or an old aunt to her: You mustn't wash it, you should only send it to the dry cleaners; have you insured it? For how much was it valued? Be careful when you get it out of your handbag!

The handkerchief itself was some eight inches by eight with another inch of intricate lace, with all the edging made in gold. In the left corner, there was the emblem of the Republic; in the right corner, the head of the Sole Leader with one printed blotch for hair, another for mouth and two round ones for eyes. The mouth looked more like a baby lizard not knowing where to go and the eyes were those of a hopeless boxer who had just received two mighty punches on both of them. But taken together with the two shrivelled ears and the square jaw, they somehow imparted a feeling of fear and rancour. Still, all the girls agreed that the image was undoubtedly that of the Sole Leader. No one could mistake it. Just under the portrait, a slogan was inscribed in Arabic: 'Who dares speaks.'

The Revolutionary Women's Federation organised a hectic programme for Miss Poran Said to visit almost every town and city in Iraq, escorted by the executives of the Federation, to demonstrate the devotion to the Sole Leader as the feminist version of true patriotism. After every speech from Mrs Wasily, Poran exhibited her handkerchief, which was then met with resounding applause and loud soprano cheers. Poran was then showered with flowers, in and out of season, and lauded with gifts ranging from the native dates, which had become so scarce in the market, to Palmolive soap, which could be found only in officers' clubs, all presented by the provincial governors, military commanders and secret police officers disguised in uniform.

This mass appreciation of her past singular gesture cultivated in her mind a frantic attachment to the golden handkerchief which accompanied her on all her travels and assignments; so much so that the people around her started to call her Miss Handkerchief, and everybody agreed that this was a better and more evocative name than the common Poran Said, which seemed to be a more appropriate name for ports and harbours as she soon found out during her first foreign trip to Egypt.

No women's delegation from Iraq was complete without Poran who attended almost every international women's event from the annual dinner of the Soroptimist International to the Conference of the World Association of Hockey Clubs. Her commitments took her to Moscow, Peking, Cairo, Paris, Prague, San Francisco and finally London.

The visit to the British capital caused great excitement in the Revolutionary Women's Federation of Iraq in view of the very special place occupied by Oxford Street in the hearts and minds of the leaders of the Arab women's liberation movement. There was considerable jostling, pushing and string-pulling in the offices of the organisation as soon as the intended visit was announced. 'Please, I need a new hip,' said the assistant secretary. 'They say they can fit you with a new hip in Harley Street.'

'And what about my vertebrae? Oh, the pain it's been giving me all these months!' said another.

'But none of you can speak English, so what is the use of you going to England? At least I can speak Armenian,' said the crafty Armenian chief clerk.

Almost crying in front of her typewriter, the Arabic typist simply moaned, 'As far as I am concerned, they can go to hell. I am not Poran; I haven't got a handkerchief to take me anywhere I want.'

'I think it's becoming ridiculous. This handkerchief has become like a holy writ from the High Kadi,' whispered another typist whilst looking carefully over her shoulder.

'I wish to God she loses it.'

'Maybe someone in London will snatch her handbag. I pray to God they may.'

The arguments of the women did not finish with the selection of the visiting delegates, but continued in the airport coach, in the jumbo jet, in the Regent Palace Hotel and in the London underground. 'You've been twice to Oxford Street today, Samira, and I haven't been there at all since Monday,' said the delegate from Basrah. 'This is unfair.'

'You know,' said Mrs Wasily to a colleague, 'You can't spend all your time in the hair-removing clinic. We have some responsibilities on this tour. Who is going to speak at the meeting tomorrow?'

But Poran was free from all this hustle and was content to spend all her time between Oxford Street and Regent Street and go back to her friends in Wimbledon Park loaded with shopping bags. After one particularly exhausting expedition, she took the Wimbledon train from the Embankment station and was immensely relieved to find an empty seat between two men. Like most of the other male passengers in the rush hour, both looked like civil servants, city brokers or business men on their way home. The one on the left of Poran was younger and spent most of the time secretly eyeing Poran out of the corner of his eye. The one on her right was an older gentleman, more formally dressed, who spent most of the time reading his newspaper and doing his best to shield himself from the presence of this exotic-looking foreign girl sitting dangerously close to him. For the latter purpose, he shifted his brief-case and put it by his side in the manner of an erected barrier between himself and the lady in question. Despite her scanty knowledge of English, Poran managed to read the business card on the briefcase: 'Royal Deodorants.' Miss Said smiled faintly as she went on wondering why the Royal family of Great Britain should sell deodorants.

This over-zealous curiosity on the part of Poran Said was detected by Mr Harrington who hastened to take additional protective measures by spreading his *Daily Telegraph* all around himself until he was almost completely wrapped up by its pages. Having thus made himself secure enough, his next move was to give all his thought and wordly concern to the printed columns all around him.

The train rumbled on from Victoria Station, to Sloane Square, to South Kensington, Gloucester Road and so on in its westerly direction towards Putney and Wimbledon, swallowing up more people and disgorging similar numbers at every station. To the young gentleman on her left, Poran appeared to have suddenly lost her serenity and comfortable posture and begun to grope for something, or struggle against something until the underground train, now travelling well overground, left Putney Bridge station to cross the River Thames. Whether it was due to a sudden gust of wind from the river escalating the perpetual draught so notoriously associated with London Transport and the British way of life, or as a result of the covetous eyes which the young gentleman was giving to the foreign-looking female sitting by his side, Poran Said could no longer suppress the onslaught of her old allergy and burst out in a violent fit of sneezing.

In the distracting confusion so typical of any allergic attack, she opened her handbag and desperately looked for the one most essential item for such an attack, and fished out the Sole Leader's handkerchief, with which she covered half of her face. Having been thus confounded and kept at bay, the draught decided to alter its tactics and within the next minute made a sudden onslaught at the elegant handkerchief, snatched it from Wahida's hands, carried it off in one gust and dropped it in

Mr Harrington's lap. It settled like a crumpled piece of paper with one corner stretching out exactly on top of his flies.

Blood rushed into Poran's face and her hand dropped by her side. Her predicament of how to rescue the precious piece of material from that delicate part of a gentleman was shared by all the fellow travellers in the train. They moved their eyes, forward and backward at her, at the handkerchief, at her shopping, at the man still barricaded behind his newspaper totally oblivious of the latest development in this underground carriage, and wondered what was best to do. A little boy who was sitting on his mother's knee made a move to jump down and rescue the misplaced item for its legitimate owner, but his mother hastened to restrain him immediately and the rebellious child only gave up the struggle after hearing a few words from his mother. She bent forward towards him and whispered what seemed like magic words in his ear. He looked at the handkerchief and the place where it had settled and then at the man, and abandoned the rescue attempt with horror clearly marked on his face.

The atmosphere engulfing that end of the carriage became so tense and delicate that even the oblivious Mr Harrington could not escape its silent demand for attention. Feeling that there was something not quite in order and that the gentlemanly act was expected of him, he lowered the newspaper a few centimetres and looked at the people on the opposite row of seats. The grinning faces were all looking in his direction and almost everyone was dying to tell him something, but were prevented by a particular air of embarrassment. As expected, Mr Harrington's immediate reaction was to blush and shiver without understanding why, what was wrong or who was guilty of anything. A furtive look at the female passenger sitting on his left revealed a very embarrassed face and a cheek going white, yellow and red in the frenzy of hurried sequences. Like the rest of the passengers around him, she was looking in his direction, or rather in the direction of his trousers just in front of his *Daily Telegraph*.

Obviously, there was something wrong – perhaps something wrong with his trousers. In a terrible moment of extreme anxiety and embarrassment clearly reflected in his twitching lips, flickering eyes and shaking hands, he lifted the newspaper stealthily and cast a casual, momentary glance down at his belt. He saw the finger of a white patch of material, and wasted no time in reaching the only logical conclusion possible for any well-groomed gentleman facing such a sight: the tail of his clean, white shirt was sticking out of his unbuttoned flies. Quick as a flash, his left hand covered his middle with the respectable *Daily Telegraph*, and with his right hand he pushed the Leader's handkerchief into his private parts. Within five seconds, he resumed his former posture with the *Daily Telegraph* all around him, reading Peterborough's 'London Day to Day'.

Mr Harrington was satisfied as he noticed that the former worried grins on the faces of his fellow travellers turned now to pleasant smiles mixed with a pinch of amusement like that of a theatre-goer coming out of a clever performance of an Oscar Wilde play, so eager to get home and tell all to the rest of the unfortunate family who missed it. Luckily for him, Mr Harrington did not cast a second furtive look at Poran, who was by then almost in tears.

At the next station, Mr Harrington folded his newspaper, picked up his briefcase and left the train. And that was how the private parts of an English gentleman happened to become the final destination of the Sole Leader's gilded portrait so dearly cherished by Miss Poran Said and her troupe of delegates from the Revolutionary Women's Federation in Iraq.

Not a very convincing tale to tell the wife.

The Cost of Old Sins

To Chris Mitchell, a retired journalist and proof reader, old age was a terrible thing and grey hair was as detestable as a mouldy banana. He had always prayed to the Almighty to spare him that misery and cut his life short and free from hearing the words 'Hello, Grandpa!' and 'Make room for the old man!' One of the most miserable days of his life was the day when a bright and pretty young woman got up and offered him her seat on the train. Oh, for the days when such a charmer used to crawl towards him and snuggle into him with lusty eyes and a big expectant smile on her ruby lips.

Most of his friends were by then either dead, bed-ridden, confined to their houses, living in nursing homes or walking with double crutches – when they could walk. Some were fortunate enough to have somebody kind enough to push them in their wheel-chairs. Yet, old friends are precious friends and they keep ringing each other and exchanging visits when-ever they could. Sylvia Burton, an artist and a graduate of Chelsea School of Arts and Crafts, was one of them, always kind, generous and faithful.

She rang him and asked him how he was and, finding that he was still alive, wanted to invite him for a light supper, for old times' sake. He was pleased to hear from that dear old romance and, finding that she was likewise still alive, wasted no time in accepting the invitation. She always cooked wonderful spaghetti Bolognese with plenty of exotic herbs.

'Do you know where I live now? I live at No 34 Elsham Road, off Holland Road in the Holland Park area. You take the Central line to Shepherd's Bush Station, turn left immediately as you leave the station and then . . . '

'Oh, you don't need to give me directions,' said he, 'I know the area well. I screwed so many women there. In fact, Sylvia my dear, I fucked the first woman I met in London on the top floor of that very house you mention, 34 Elsham Road, when I came down from Yorkshire. I won't be a stranger to it. I used to pay for it two pounds and ten pence per week. Sex was, of course, free of charge but not the gas and electricity.'

'Oh, you!'

Chris rang the bell of that memorable love nest and Sylvia came limping painfully, walking step by step with the help of two aluminium crutches. They kissed and hugged warmly, with her grey eyes moistening as she led the old friend into her small flatlet consisting of one small bedroom, an open plan kitchen/sitting room and a tiny bathroom with a shower. They sat on the only two available cane

chairs and listened to the usual saga of hospitals and hip operations. What went wrong and what should have been done but was overlooked by the medics. She just managed to open the one door of the small pine cupboard and brought out the old bottle of Chianti, still in its straw nest.

'Darling, you open it for us,' she said as she handed him the bottle and the corkscrew. 'Your hand is stronger than mine. Lucky that you are here to do that for me.'

'Not in the least. I can't use my hand nowadays for anything. I'll spill the precious wine if I try. Look! Look, darling. See how my hand is shaking and trembling all the time.'

'How come? You used to have such a strong hand.'

'I think it is the result of spending all my life writing, especially when there were no computers. We had to use our hands, pen and paper. Twenty-five books took their toll. Writing consumed the nerves and muscles of my wrist and my fingers.'

While opening the wine bottle by herself, old Sylvia thought for a while, smiled with a mischievous grin and said, 'No, Chris dear. I know what happened to your fingers and your right wrist. Too much fingering into ladies' cleavages. Hours of titillating excited clits destroyed your middle finger.' She coughed and coughed as she laughed and added, 'You are paying for it now, darling. Trembling hands. An awful tremor! God's punishment on you!'

'I don't think so. What about my tongue then? It is completely OK. I am still lecturing and broadcasting and talking to you. Nothing happened to the muscles of my tongue. I think I used it even more than I used my middle finger. Yet it is still in a very sound state. I give my weekly radio talks without any problem. Only last month I spoke for probably a whole hour at the Conference on International Terrorism. You see, here I am talking to you without the slightest hitch. Absolutely nothing wrong with my tongue. Or my mouth.'

'I don't know. But Dr Helena Stephens, you remember her, the one you used to screw after tennis, said to my ex-boyfriend, Muhammad Wali, that this kind of hand tremor could be the result of too much masturbation in his teens.'

It didn't take Chris Mitchell long to change the conversation and respond in kind. 'Now listen, Sylvy my dear, I can also tell you how you have got this trouble with your legs. You strained your hips so often and so badly in opening your legs so high and so wide for any randy invader, big or small. Hips were not made for such wild fucking as you used to give. You never gave your slim pelvis time to rest and recover. Never put your legs down and closed them. You are paying now for your old sins, my dear.'

'No, I don't agree with you, Chris. I don't accept your diagnosis at all, what you say about the causes of my trouble, because most of the time that you have in mind, your dirty mind, I was simply bending on my knees in the doggy position anyway, my favourite position.'

'That can be even worse for the cartilage of the knees and the spine. Anyway, have you tried some physiotherapy?'

'Of course I did. What do you think? The physiotherapist cost me almost a thousand pounds. None of the exercises he gave me made any difference. These people are crooks and sharks.'

'I tell you what though. Listen to me now carefully. The best exercise for this kind of trouble, backache and leg pain, is swimming. But the next best exercise is sexual intercourse. What is so good about it is that it mixes the physical with the emotional, the pain with the pleasure. And that is half the battle. The Arabs have a saying for it. They say, "Treat your trouble with the cause of the trouble." Take my advice and indulge as best as . . .'

'What are you talking about? I tell you I can't even move my legs and you tell me to have more sex. How am I to do that?'

'You don't need to open or raise your legs. You know that. I shall bring you an illustrated Japanese sex manual showing you forty-eight positions, twenty-five for vaginal sex and eighteen for anal sex and the rest for lesbian, all graphically illustrated in the old Yamato-e style. Choose what suits you best and give your legs more mobility and exercise.'

Sylvia dismissed Mr Mitchell's advice with a burst of denigrating laughter. 'No, my love. I tell you what. You choose the position which may put some life in your own penis!'

It was his turn to burst out laughing. He pulled her towards him and showered her shrivelled cheeks and thin lips with kisses which she heartily accepted and enjoyed. This was followed by a long pause of pensive silence during which Sylvia lit a second cigarette and had another big gulp of the good old red wine whilst Chris raised his half-closed eyes to look at the ceiling.

It is very true. Old people spend most of their remaining time on earth reminiscing about the good old days when a woman could be sure that the man had the burning desire and the ability to match.

It was past midnight when they finished eating all that was there on the table, the spaghetti, the green salad, Cheddar cheese and black olives, and drank the last drop of the Chianti. It was time for the old gentleman to take his leave and bid the old friend good-night. She picked up her two steel crutches and he helped her to her feet. 'Ouch!' They walked slowly to the front door where the old couple, one time young lovers, exchanged a few tender kisses and hugged each other gently.

'All in all, and whatever we may say, I think it was really worth it. Wasn't it, darling?'

For Love and Money

On the outskirts of the new city of Hillah by the old city of Babylon, just where the tourists make their entry and the natives squat patiently waiting for the deluge, lived Hasnah, a middle-aged maiden who earned her living by the collection and sale of firewood. Although she lived alone, Hasnah was not really lonely for she had a nice, contented she-donkey which had been her pet, companion and source of living ever since she moved into town. Her donkey had always been such a sympathetic animal. Whenever it looked from its stable through the unglazed window into the bedroom of its proprietress, it felt deep compassion for the old maid in this man-dominated land. It often grabbed a mouthful of grass and put its head through the bedroom door. Muhra, as she was called, possessed great philosophical sense, rare even among the families of the wise donkeys of Babylon.

With the deterioration of the international monetary system and effective devaluation of the Eurodollar, Muhra was no longer able to cope with the rising cost of living and presented her mistress with a real test of her intelligence and ingenuity. Thank God Muhra was a she-ass. If she could be induced to produce and propagate her species, Hasnah would have two donkeys instead of one. The difficulty was that Hasnah could not spare the one dinar for the professional people with the professional male donkeys. If only she could contrive a rendezvous for Muhra! Yet a rendezvous was more than Hasnah had ever succeeded in arranging for her own self.

It was on a spring afternoon when Hasnah struck on the idea. She was squatting on the one step outside her house with nobody to interrupt her thoughts. The heat of the day could be felt on the bricks of the step as if some genie was cooking human flesh underneath. Although there was no vegetation where Hasnah lived, and dirty, soapy water flowed freely through the ditches on both sides of the road, day and night, one could still smell the heavy, sweet scent of the famous Baghdad roses gently carried by the west wind from the distant garden of the government, its bureaucrats, their cousins and their brothers-in-law. April was indeed in the air. No one could tell whether it was all sheer materialism on Hasnah's part or something to do with those illusive sparks of life and desire firing her imagination with the same vigour with which she was gulping the spoonfuls of rice from the earthenware bowl in her hand.

Hasnah just sat by her doorstep watching the shabby passers-by and flicking away the hungry flies as big as old men's spit and as noisy and persistent as twenty beggars at a Muslim funeral. It was a long time since she had remembered her dead father and the small village from which she came. How many times he had spoiled definite proposals for her, how he had disposed of all the best suitors, people who did not live with donkeys and fodder but owned lorries and came from the world of grease and additive oils. She remembered the few girls who managed to elope and have their heads severed in houses of ill fame. A secret admiration came over her.

Her thoughts came to a dead stop as the silence was interrupted by the jingling bells of the donkey pulling the rubbish cart of Jabbar, the dustman, and his shrill cry, 'Ekhdi! Son of an infidel.'

'Shame on you, Jabbar, hitting a poor animal which doesn't understand,' Hasnah protested.

Jabbar did not as much as cast a glance at her, but he replied, instead, by swishing his stick in the air once more and hitting his animal even harder: 'Ekhdi, son of an infidel!' The donkey responded by making a sudden jolt which pulled the rubbish cart a long way from where the dustman wanted it. There was a trail of broken glass, old newspapers, mouldy pieces of bread and miscellaneous unwanted items left behind. Jabbar raised both arms to God and opened his mouth to utter some genuinely original, unheard-of curses. His lips remained parted like those of an opera singer in a silent movie. Eventually he simply collapsed and fell to his knees right in the middle of the narrow thoroughfare, sitting like a statue of utter despair, a pose which his own donkey would have loved to make but was obviously not allowed to.

'God will smite you one day for ill-treating his creations,' Hasnah said as she walked to the cart, collecting the strewn pieces on her way, and ad-monished the poor animal gently – 'You have been naughty, you know' – and with a tender tap on its rump she led it back to her doorstep where water from cool earthenware was brought for it. Jabbar, by this time on his feet again, had his share as well and had even a bit from the rice bowl from which Hasnah was eating.

The house soon became a halting place for Jabbar and his ass. Water, and often rice and bread as a second course, was served in the shade. Hasnah introduced her own she-ass to the party discreetly, and the dustman showed his own generosity by diving his hand into the pile of rubbish and fishing out a few thick, juicy peelings of water melon. The two donkeys loved that and enjoyed the whole affair to the full. Jabbar's donkey snatched a piece occasionally from Muhra's mouth and made off with it. That was the furthest point he reached in his recognition of Muhra. Animals do not seem to be sociable creatures, Hasnah thought. She tried her best to present Muhra in the most favourable light. Sometimes she brought her over in full costume – best new saddle and shining plastic reins. She polished her brass bells and hung them onto a scarlet rope with chrysanthemum-like flowers made of dyed Kurdish wool and in colours not shown in the most comprehensive botanical encyclopaedia. On other occasions she brought Muhra as God made her, so to speak, nude and naked but washed and brushed.

Yet all to no avail! The brute had been for donkey's years in the service of the government, and had nearly become a broken civil servant himself. He just carried out his instructions, ate his water melon peelings, drank his bucket of cool water and gazed blankly at the wall in front of him, waiting for orders. At the slightest mew of a cat he pricked up his ears, thinking it was meant for him. After long pauses of dead silence and immobility, he would look around, make sure that nobody was watching him and then move one of his limbs a few inches forward into the publicly owned grounds. The pace being such a strain on him he would close his eyes in exhaustion and simply doze, albeit standing with full harness in the middle of his working day and at a short distance from a senior boss. A few moments would pass and then another mew from a cat would startle him. He would jump in extreme worry and excitement, run around himself, kick the bucket of water, wet and soil the publicly owned ground and make an utter misery of himself.

Unlike his animal, Jabbar made better friends. Instead of restricting himself to the narrow brick step, he ventured inside and started to have his rest and daily chat in Hasnah's multi-purpose room. There he sat on the floor and discussed with his hostess the latest republican decrees and the rising cost of petitions.

'My donkey is an Arab. Do you think yours is a Kurd or a Turk?' Jabbar simply replied by shrugging his shoulders.

'They don't seem to get on easily. There are Kurdish and Turkish donkeys, you know. There are even English and German donkeys, they say.'

Jabbar simply mumbled in reply, 'There are blasted donkeys everywhere.'

'These two are such good animals. If only we could get them mating. How do people do such things, Jabbar? I mean do it between . . . my meaning is to get the animals . . . you know my meaning.'

The dustman dropped his plate of rice. 'So that is what it is. That is your sort of kindness and hospitality. I should have known better. Everyone is looking after his own interests in this world, isn't he?'

'But we are not doing any harm . . . '

'No harm at all! The municipal donkey of the Rubbish Disposal Department seduced and misused, exploited, exhausted, his energy sapped! You call it no harm at all. Oh, not me, not me, weakening the government's ass.'

'But he will soon recover, dear Jabbar. Besides, it is all natural. The poor thing must be so frustrated.'

'Frustrated! That is the word! And why shouldn't he be? It is obvious. Animals come first in the world.'

Now Hasnah could only turn her face away from Jabbar's fixed eyes. She looked at the ground and gradually towards the empty stable of Muhra.

'I shall not have the government's donkey abused, not me, not even for money.'

There he gave Hasnah her cue. After some hard bargaining it was agreed that Jabbar would prevail on his donkey and would receive half a dinar once all was well. The date was fixed. But what if the municipal donkey stuck to the letter and spirit of his contract of employment? What if half a dinar or a full dinar were all one to him and he refused to show any enthusiasm for the task? These were questions which shrewd Hasnah had to consider. She had not lived all these years by herself and preserved her life and chastity against all odds for nothing.

'By Allah, you accuse the government's donkey of impotence? Oh, if the Chief Inspector heard that!'

Hasnah was not swayed by such an assurance and Jabbar had to prove that his donkey was as good as her silver.

In the same ramshackle district lived an old turbaned oracle who arbitrated between the people, married them for a few dirhams and then divorced them for a lesser amount. He healed their children, beat them, bailed them out of prison and collected their wages. He invested the people's money and made a mockery of all state departmental demarcations. To him Jabbar and Hasnah went. The shaikh, as he was called, had a grey beard, polished boots, clean clothes, a Biro ballpoint pen stuck in his breast pocket – and all that smacked of authority. Hasnah's ten dirhams plus two for his own labour were thrust in his hand. They would only be delivered on such a date and hour as fixed between the two parties and on the personal satisfaction of the old man that the performance was correct and fruitful to the best capabilities and experience of the Municipal donkey.

No one could have believed that Jabbar had such a wealth of knowledge on this subject. It surprised all witnesses. Hasnah was simply thrilled and the old man chuckled with approval as Jabbar rolled up his sleeves, got hold of the hem of his long, white gown, put it in his mouth for no obvious reason whatsoever and then stuffed it under his wide, leather belt just below the navel and, with his legs completely exposed, looked as if he were going to perform the deed himself. He hurried to his donkey, freed him from the cart, unharnessed him in no time and did all kinds of tricks which amused all the onlookers who, by this time, were by no means a few.

Both animals were manifestly new to the affair.

Anxious and bewildered, the male donkey was even more mortified by his illiteracy which made it impossible for him to pick up a newspaper and pretend that he was busy reading. Muhra closed her eyes and, like any she-ass of good breeding and class, preferred to assume that she didn't know what was happening. From time to time, she opened one eye slightly and cast a look at Jabbar who was howling with monosyllables which neither man nor beast could understand. In the excitement and tension of the moment, the municipal donkey failed in the entrusted task and sacred mission of Mother Nature. Jabbar kicked the poor animal with utmost disgust and fury. Bending forward, the dustman stretched his hands and, almost piously touching the ground, he gasped, 'The government's seed's gone to earth!'

This was quite an unexpected turn of events. The donkey is weakened but Muhra is not mated. Everybody turned to the old shaikh. What was going to happen to the ten dirhams? The venerable shaikh put a hand in his pocket and made sure that the money was still there. He stroked his grey beard many times, thoughtfully, whilst the crowd around him argued most learnedly and with the best legal jargon learnt from the television political trials of little different nature or results. When the tumult died down, he walked to Jabbar's donkey and looked him in the face attentively before making his pronouncement: 'The case is obvious. The beast is degenerate. It is a nationalised beast. It is a government donkey.'

To keep any further argument at bay, he added, 'Man, we give you seven days to make amends. Take your donkey away and bring him back when he is fitter for the job again.'

The dustman was very anxious to get his money and spent the next few days feeding his donkey with such animal aphrodisiacs as old dates mixed with mahogany sawdust and dry red clover soaked in sour camel milk – the two recipes highly recommended by Shaikh Wali al-Barthuli in his *Ninety-nine Love Acts of Hooved Animals*, dedicated to his eunuch Sultan Abdul Latif with ample citations from scriptures. The effectiveness of the rare recipe acted like magic in less than a week as Jabbar could see plainly from the sudden eagerness of the animal, and a second rendezvous was therefore arranged forthwith.

Reins undone, saddle taken off, the victim was brought for the ordeal once more. It was an even hotter afternoon, for the short spring of Iraq was rapidly giving way to the cruel sun of the never-ending summer. With his gown tucked once more under his belt, Jabbar went to his task with all agility and determination. The scorching asphalt road did not affect his bare feet. The bearded old man, though his hands were quite empty, looked as if he was holding a stop watch this time. One or two children held stones in their hands ready to hurl them at anyone and any beast who proved to be a spoilsport. Some women who also stood by and pretended not to see, protested:

'Why, upon my soul! This is haram. It's sacrilege! Here on the public road where people kneel and make their prayers!'

'Why don't they go to the police station? They can do it there.'

'What about the school? That's an even better place. They do this sort of thing there all the time.'

No one listened to them and none of them went away. The donkey showed that he had benefited immensely from the experience of life and the seven days diet. Everything was going tip-top when suddenly all attention was diverted towards the bellowing horn of a motor vehicle. A khaki-coloured van wanted some room to pass. Somebody rushed to the abandoned cart which rested on its back with its two shafts pointing upwards like a pair of barrels. They pushed it sideways to the wall. A thoroughfare was made for the traffic, but the van did not move. Its door opened and a man in uniform and wearing a peaked cap with a sizeable badge, stepped out.

'The Chief Inspector!' the crowd murmured, some of them disappearing hastily. The donkey was instantly emasculated and started pacing away sideways. The inspector was a fat, round man with a moustache just like his badge, grossly exaggerated.

As soon as he faced the crowd he took off his peaked cap, obviously not out of respect but because of the heat. His bald head reflected the glare of the sun like an antique, copper mirror. He stared at his dustman, at the spectacle, the abandoned cart, the children with the stones still ready in hand and then at his dustman again.

'A very fine job indeed!' said he. 'The property of the government misused and with the full cooperation of its own employee. I should like to know how you are going to account for this tomorrow.'

Jabbar replied, 'It is only to increase the population, effendi.'

But the Chief Inspector was a man of authority and was not easily swayed. He was used to the world of patriotic words. 'Very true, very true – increase the population! A very good reason, by the soul of the Prophet! Weaken the donkey of the Rubbish Disposal Department with sex and promiscuity! A very fine thing and a very fine reason! I hope you won't forget that tomorrow. You will have to tell more about it to the cashier when you draw your outstanding wages, if you still deserve them. The Immortal Republic has no need for people who show no consideration to its animals.'

The Chief Inspector put on his cap again, got back into his van and drove away, leaving behind a cloud of dust which submerged everything. The game was over. The two creatures, the properties of the private sector and the public sector of the republic's mixed economy, had to be separated immediately and Muhra was led indoors disappointed, kicking everything in her way.

'I knew nothing would come of it,' said the local schoolmaster who had joined the crowd during the last minutes. 'Fancy crossing a nationalised donkey with a privately owned she-ass! What kind of a foal are you going to get?'

Jabbar did not finish his day's work. Instead of continuing his round, he drove his animal into Hasnah's stable. Throughout the night he held conference with her. Notes were exchanged and compared. They covered wide parts of their lives, and examined the present in the light of the inspector's words. The old shaikh, who joined them, reminded them of the Martial Law and the Revolutionary Court.

'I've seen them with my own eyes,' said the old shaikh solemnly, 'hanging a man for importing a parrot which said Salam alaykum in Hebrew.'

Just before the call to the dawn prayer was heard from the giant loudspeaker hugging the nearest minaret like a black devil laughing his belly out at those within hearing, the situation was resolved and a carefully constructed plan was hammered out. When the sun was rising the following day over the straight horizon and illuminating the golden tops of the sacred domes and lofty minarets, it cast long shadows behind four creatures in great haste. They were pushing forward to the edge of the desert. The two donkeys, loaded with what was worth the trouble, travelled side by side like two old companions happily rejoined. Hasnah and Jabbar were spurring them on, looking behind all the time. 'Ekhdi! Son of an infidel!'

Behind them, back where Hasnah had lived for many years, the donkey cart remained standing in its place with its full load still on and its two shafts pointing upwards. It soon became a familiar sight and children stopped climbing it and beggars likewise gave up rummaging in it. Throughout the neighbourhood, the story spread from mouth to mouth: 'Old Hasnah has eloped with the government's donkey.'

Fairuz

Fairuz was a very promising young woman from Morocco: beautiful brown face, smooth like a giant chestnut, tall, slim figure and an enchanting voice with a singing ability to match. She had an extensive repertoire covering songs from practically all Arab countries, a very rare accomplishment indeed. No other artist could beat her when she accompanied her North African songs with her native Berber dancing of the Atlas mountains. I tried unsuccessfully to promote her and wrote a couple of articles in al-Sharq al-Awsat about her singing and dancing talent. But fate wouldn't have it. I introduced her to some TV producers and cabaret impresarios, but they all simply ravished her and threw her out in the morning empty handed, so to speak. She eventually came to the conclusion that she might as well go the whole hog and earn some money out of all this shameful rigmarole. Why give it free when she could at least charge for it? With a little bit of advice from wiser people, she was directed to join the hordes of Arab hookers in Edgware Road, London.

No money to be earned out of me, we parted ways

for a good many years as I wished her good luck in her new career. In the meantime she made some good money and bought a luxury flat in Kensington and a comfortable home to house her wretched family back in Marrakech, whilst I achieved some prominence in my less rewarding career of writing.

Later, I was puzzled and rather annoyed by her late telephone calls at night, sometimes past midnight when I was preparing to sleep.

'Hi Khalid, how are you? Haven't seen you for a long time. Any new books you published? Oh, how thoughtless of you! Not sending me a copy! I shall cry. You don't love me. You don't care for me any more!'

All these niceties would go on for a minute or two and then she would bid me good night and ring off. This repeated rigmarole intrigued me. Why did she always ring me at those late hours, often waking me up from my deep sleep, when she had the whole day to speak to me?

I grumbled about it to my friend and colleague, Abdul Razzaq, a more knowledgeable man than me in these matters. It didn't take us long to conclude that she did so whenever she was with some rich Arab Gulf client. I had attained some popularity as a humour columnist among the Gulf peoples. 'Oh, you know Khalid Kishtainy, that great writer! Fancy that! How do you know him, tell us.' She would then pick up the telephone and repeat that conversation about neglecting her and not sending her my latest book. They would immediately change their tone and their manners in dealing with her. They stop mauling her whilst she was eating her kebab and homous or asking her to do any thing perverted. They certainly topped up her fees as a high class mistress who knew famous writers like Khalid Kishtainy. Even more to the point, they would go back to their country in the Arab Gulf, Kuwait, Dubai or Qatar, and recommend her to their relatives and business colleagues. 'Going to London? Oh London! My dear! That great city! Take my advice! Don't mess about with low class street walkers in Soho. Go straight to the Kishtainy whore in Edgware Road. Ask any of our staff at our Embassy about where to find her. They all know her place well. She is a bit more expensive, but, oh my dear! She'll tell you so much about our beloved Khalid Abu Niall. She knows him well.'

I don't mind Fairuz (her professional name, of course), earning more money and having more oil rich clientele, but am I not entitled to some portion of her earnings out of her use of my name? Isn't that part of free market ethics? I live by my pen as a word worker and she lives by her body as a sex worker, albeit I might prefer to call her, as I knew her well, a sex artist rather than a mere hum-drum sex worker. I think I should be entitled to a certain proportion of every fee she receives per encounter.

I am thinking now of seeking the advice of a good solicitor with enough experience in such delicate business matters. I don't want to be prosecuted for living off the immoral earnings of a woman, legal or illegal immigrant, but an author's name is a commodity protected by law. I don't want any silly Salma or tubby Fatima to play around with it whilst another man is impregnating her. I should also be entitled to compensations for the stress I had to endure whilst sitting in my gloomy study room surrounded by my heavy books and hateful dictionaries receiving a telephone call to tell me that another luckier man is having a glorious time with that lovely young woman, Fairuz. Surely a British court of justice would take cognisance under English Law of this mental suffering and emotional frustration I have to endure and allow me a fair proportion of her charges as compensation as well as professional fees for the use of my name.

Good Abdul Razzaq agreed with me and even recommended for me a City solicitors firm to call on and seek their advice. 'But Abu Niall, how are you going to ascertain the right amount due to you from this so called Fairuz and her sex activities? Hard enough to trust an Arab politician in what they say, let alone an Arab whore. I tell you what. You should look for a good electronic meter to fix on her sex organs to record every entry and every exit with the correct duration involved. You read the meter by the end of every month and work out what is rightly due to you. As a good Muslim, you must never forget what the Holy Qur'an says. God is just and loves those who walk along the path of justice and righteousness.'

Talking of Organs

When Um Ghafur, wife of Maitre Saad Kadir, walked along with her inseparable butch companion, Ms Alia Abdul Wahid, school mistress at the Bardudia Primary School for Girls in the Toub district, in the direction of the Midan bazaar, they passed by the sprawling Defence coffee house. It was so called not for any part it had ever played in defence of the country or indeed in anything, but simply because it happened to be situated at Baghdad's main thorough-fare, the notable Rashid Street, just opposite the Ministry of Defence, which made it a natural haunt for army officers playing backgammon and dominoes all day long. The café was, as usual, full of customers, all of the male sex, whiling away the time by playing games or chatting and shouting. As the two ladies passed by, Um Ghafur could no longer resist this irksome question which had bothered her for a good many years. She turned to her companion, the school teacher, Alia, and asked her: 'Tell me, dear – these men sitting in this smoky café all day and night talking – what do they talk about all the time?'

'Why, darling, what do you think they talk about?

They have nothing to talk about other than your "capital" "malik" and my *capital* "mali".'

What this respectable primary school teacher meant in her local Iraqi dialect by 'capital' was the sexual organ, or what is euphemistically put in the Holy Qur'an as the 'farg' or the cleavage. It was a very appropriate and clever expression, for a woman's sexual organ in that part of the globe is indeed her only real asset and capital in this world. Well used, it can raise the status of the most wretched street pedlar or orange seller to the rank of a minister or a prominent lady rolling in riches. Stupidly used and abused, it would only lead her to the dagger or bullet of the honour cleanser, be that her father, brother, husband or any kinsman, however near or far. She was right in what was usually talked about in the café, but at that point in time she was wrong, for the group of middle-aged men sitting around the table facing the ramshackle pavement outside, and who attracted her attention and inspired the fair comment, were not discussing her 'capital' or her friend's 'capital' but rather their own 'capital'.

They met daily at this café and took up their positions, always at this corner to watch more closely any female creature passing by and make their sound comments. Abu Lutfi, the former clerk at the Passport Office who was sacked for failing to share his bribes with his boss, did not, however, attend this regular gathering for two days. His friends were worried. He might have been arrested and sent to the Abu Ghraib's concentration camp, they thought, or perhaps shot dead outside his house in one of those endless 'acts of God'. God became very busy with these acts in this period of the Revolution.

'Where have you been, Abu Lutfi? You made us very worried about you. We thought of calling on you to enquire, but in the end we told ourselves – better not. You know how things are. Still, tell us. We hope all is well.'

'Oh, yes. All is well, thanks be to Allah. Nothing wrong at all. I felt as if I was catching the 'flu or something and decided to stay in bed until I was alright. But I was wrong. There was nothing the matter with me. No 'flu, cold or anything.'

'Strange! How on earth did you think you were going to get influenza? Do you have a radar monitoring the approach of germs?'

'Oh, yes indeed. I have such a radar – a foolproof radar. It is my penis, pardon the expression. Like most men, I am used to waking up just before dawn. I get my sleep interrupted by my *capital*. I find it erect and strong like steel, eager for action. It remains so for one or two hours, depriving me totally from sleep until it gets fed up with me, gives up hope and shrinks and goes back to sleep. With that, I resume my own sleeping peacefully.'

'That is right, my dear Abu Lutfi. All men have the same problem. Sometimes the penis refuses to relax and go back to sleep until the unhappy man is forced to grab his poor woman, sleeping soundly as she might be by his side, and give her one. This is what is called the dawn intercourse. It is a good one. The best. Our divines say that the dawn intercourse is blessed by the Almighty. The offspring would be strong and healthy. There is also more fun and enjoyment in it, because it has God's own blessings on it for as soon as the work is done, the man gets up, does the ablutions and makes his dawn prayer. It is a blessed intercourse loved by the Almighty. At least that is how it used to be. But people nowadays think of nothing other than the fuck and forget all about God and the dawn prayers.'

Having heard these wise observations from Major General Hamid al-Dabshuli, twice decorated with the Rafidain Medal for Valour, Abu Lutfi resumed his narrative.

'You are right, General. So, a couple of days passed without me waking up at night at all. My *capital* made no attempt to raise its head and arouse me. It never swelled or got any erection. Why is that? How comes? I knew I was in for some kind of trouble – some virus, some illness that hit me.'

Here, the retired civil servant was once more interrupted by Major General al-Dabshuli, who had developed a totally different means of diagnosis. 'Yes, what you say may be quite correct for you, my dear friend, but I personally can always recognise

the imminent attack of a cold from my shoulders. As soon as I feel a chill in my shoulders at the back, I know I am going to have a cold. I immediately get out my woollen jumpers and keep myself warm.'

Like all Iraqis bent on contradicting each other, Maitre Abdul Hussain Mutlaq hastened to put a different point of view. 'No, no, no, not the shoulders. It is the legs. When you feel your legs aching, be one hundred per cent sure that you are going to get influenza. Look to your legs. This is what the old proverb says: "Fever comes from your feet." Remember the song of Aziz Ali: "Al humma tijina min rejlayna" (Fever comes from our feet). This is what I always say. Keep your feet warm and your head cool.'

'My experiences tell me,' Ali Nufal, a wheat merchant from Basrah, interposed, 'that it is not the shoulders or the legs which signal the approach of a nasty cold, but the throat. As soon as you feel a tickle there, some sore spot, take a couple of aspirins and go to bed immediately. Keep yourself warm and drink lots of hot drinks. Grab your woman under the blanket and warm yourself with her bottom. Take my word. Nothing keeps a man warm on a cold night then the bottom of a truly plump woman, round and fleshy. The two solid buttocks of a Kurdish lady from Sulaymania are worth ten Aladdin stoves in winter.'

The discussion went on among this happy group of old friends about sickness and health, what symptoms, what remedies, how best to recognise diabetes, ulcers, high blood pressure, heart trouble, etc. Someone referred to his interrupted sleep, another thought it was the other way around, that is, excessive tendency to fatigue and sleep. Shaikh Abdul Rahim Agha spoke about his experiences with his stomach ulcer. Whenever he felt he must eat something outside the normal time of meals, he knew his ulcer was starting again. All was not well. But Abu Lutfi resumed his analysis.

'Oh, good people, believe you me, by the Almighty Allah who gathered us around here and will re-gather us on his Day of Judgement, I tell you. All this talk about your shoulders, legs, feet, throats and what have you is irrelevant. Forget them all and keep your eyes on your penis. It is your most accurate barometer. Watch him. He is your good and free guide. He monitors and responds to anything going on inside you. Whenever I have something amiss, he shrinks and rejects any attempt to arouse him. I haven't finished my story yet. What I have learnt also was to look at his behaviour as an indicator of my condition and the progress of my illness. When I am not well, I cannot even find him to pass water. He is no longer in this world. He doesn't exist. But as soon as I see some life in him, swelling and raising his head, I know the treatment is working. My quack has done a good job. Believe you me, you can test your condition and the progress of your treatment from the firmness and eagerness of your willy. Take a ruler and measure its length carefully as it extends and write it down in your notebook. You get a good idea of the extent of your recovery from that simple record.'

'Like a thermometer.'

'Oh, Abu Abdullah, better than any thermometer, barometer or what have you.'

The truth is that not only Abu Lutfi made this useful discovery, but also his wife, Um Lutfi who, over the years of sharing the same bed, noticed the same scientific phenomenon. In her turn, whenever she was awakened by Abu Lutfi's hard instrument pressing and prodding into her side, her thigh or her bottom she knew that her husband was OK, brimming with good health. She would smile contentedly and say one or two words of thanks to the merciful and compassionate God for looking after the wellbeing of this family. But woe to her if she woke up and found nothing pressing on her side in that strategic part of her anatomy. She would then stretch her arm under the blanket and look for it because sometimes it could be concealed between her husband's legs or stretching between the big folds of his fat belly. Once found, strong, fully blown and extended to its full length, she would feel reassured and cite a verse or two of blessings from the Holy Qur'an: 'Remember thou God's bounties upon you if Him thou doth worship.' This said, she would then pull back her hand, wipe it with the bed sheets and leave his willy in peace. Um Lutfi would then turn to the other side of the double iron bed and go back to sleep. If, for whatever reason, she happened to find it contracted and lying limp over his testicles like a stale and short runner bean or small mouldy piece of okra, she would be overwhelmed with anxiety and spend the rest of the night with her eyes wide open, waiting for the early hours of the morning, praying all the time for some holy saint or some descendant of the Prophet with a green turban to intervene and restore her husband's thing to full erection and good health in mercy for this poor family in those unhappy days of shortages and UN sanctions and all those bastards of the Ba'th Party lurking on every street corner.

Sometimes, she could not bear it any longer and would wake up her husband with a nudge into his stomach or a gentle pull of his penis. 'Darling, Abu Lutfi, apple of my eye, what is the matter with you, eh? Something wrong? God forbid! Tell me darling, habibi, why is it so?' She would give it another pull. 'Why so limp and lifeless? Go and see the doctor.'

Abu Lutfi went on advising his friends and urging them to keep a good watch over their penises. 'Since I discovered this fact of life, I've never lost sight of my *capital.* I don't care at all for what goes on in the rest of my body, leg, heart, kidneys, liver, whatever. These are all secondary items, and nowadays replaceable.

As long as I wake at three or four in the morning with a full erection, with my *capital* hard and strong, its head upright and ready for attack, I know I am all right. I am told that even some scientists in the United States started to check the health of their president by the duration of his penis's erection at night. This is a matter on which world peace depends. They brought him a Jewish consultant from Tel Aviv to monitor the state of his penis. Never mind the election, they said, watch over the erection. This is what President Clinton was doing. Monica was checking on the state of his willy.'

The discussion went forward and backward, this way and that way, with plenty of reminiscences, references, citation of verses and proverbs, what Plato had said, al-Farrabi and Avicenna, what the old divinities and doctors had written about the sexual organs, coitus, erotic desires, descriptions of penises and vaginas, their categories and complexions. What is good and desirable in them, or detestable and unappetising. What men prefer and what women desire. Major General al-Dabshuli dwelt on the subject of length and size. Did it really matter? But anyway, was it the length or width which made the difference for women? Shaikh Abdul Rahim touched on the subject of boys and how their anuses could be easily torn and damaged by oversized ones and unmindful fisting.

All in all, school mistress Alia Aabdul Wahid's

notion that this group of men were discussing her *capital* and her companion's *capital* was totally wrong. They were indeed discussing their own *capitals*. Thus they started their evening and thus they concluded their session. They rose to settle their account with the café owner, Said Abdul Azim, and bade each other good night.

'Have a good sleep. And you, Abu Lutfi, we wish you well. May the Almighty Allah bless your *capital* tonight with a good erection. He is the most powerful and all compassionate.'

The men dispersed to their own homes at Sabunchia, al-Toub or Bab al-Muadam as the case might have been. They just parted for the night like all Middle Eastern men, only to meet the following day at the same place, same time, to start all over again, drink their Turkish coffee or tea – sweet as syrup – and smoke their favourite hubble-bubble. Mr Wali Abu Lutfi appeared once more with the evening newspaper under his arm.

'Salam alykum, my friends.'

'And alykum al-Salam. Hope you are well today, Abu Lutfi. How did you feel last night? How was your *capital*? In good shape, I hope. Strong and alert like a python?'

'Just like a rod of iron, solid like steel, Abu Abdulla.'

'Praise be to Allah! There is no power except from the Almighty.'

DEDICATION

The foregoing story is dedicated to my GP, Dr Peter Tudor Miles and all the medical practitioners in the Wimbledon Village Surgery who always ask their patients – do they smoke, do they drink, do they sleep well, any pain? How often do they pass water? What colour is their shit? But they never ask them about their sexual life and how often do they fuck. Something is missing in British medicine.

Pioneers of the Cooperative Movement

It is generally believed that the cooperative movement has no history or tradition in Iraq and the whole Arab world, other than the scanty and corrupt co-operative societies set up by the authorities mainly to satisfy the Western observers and open new fields for robbing the state as well as the poor peasants and labourers. Yet the old story of Jabbar the Lame, Hassun the Blind and Fahima the Dumb denies this impression. They all lived in the depressed district of Bab al-Sheikh which had the highest number of blind and dumb people and was, indeed, in competition with the nearby district of Bab alagha in the number of those who lost the use of their legs in a country where legs are all that matters for running away from the police and running after any morsel of food, edible or inedible. Bab al-Sheikh attracted such people because of the presence of the great al-Ghazali cemetery and its thousands of ramshackle graves reminding the passers-by of the impending doom and the Day of Judgement. It was the best place to make people part with their money and share a handful of it with the poor who were privileged with the loss of their sight, sound and limbs. Bab alagha, on the other hand, had the advantage of the noisy Copper Market, Suq al-Safafir, with its metal workers banging loud on something or other the whole day long, a very congenial environment for the deaf and dumb of the country.

Jabbar the Lame lost his legs as a result of climbing over the wall to steal a look at the neighbour's women when they were relieving themselves in the open. The sight must have been so overwhelming to the young man that he lost balance, fell and broke his right leg, a good lesson for the breakers of the traditional respect to female neighbours. Baghdad's only professional bone setter had his practice in Suq al-Safafir, the great Copper Market, as the cries and screams of the victims are drowned by the louder noise of metal bashing.

The unfortunate sinner was taken to the copper worker-bone setter to have his leg repaired. After two months of painful pulling and twisting, the leg was repaired but, alas, some three centimetres short of its original length, which made it difficult for Jabbar to walk evenly or painlessly. All the well-meaning neighbours blamed him. 'Silly man! Why did you go to this old-fashioned fellow, a mere copper smith? Why didn't you go to the new Royal Hospital? There is an English surgeon there now. He can cure anything and measures things with a ruler.'

Dr S. D. Atkins was waiting for him in his white gown. Unfamiliar with the metric system, he assumed that the report in hand was referring to three inches. To make the two legs equal, he picked up his saw and knives and cut three inches from the left leg. The right leg became now four centimetres longer than the left leg making it even more difficult for Jabbar to walk steadily. Back to the hospital he was taken only to discover that Dr Atkins was no longer there as he found things quite confusing in this Muslim country and returned to England where people didn't use the metric system. An Armenian doctor who studied medicine in Istanbul during the Ottoman era took over. He could not understand one single word in the Arabic report. 'Don't worrying me, effendi! Me sets you right,' he said to him in broken Arabic He took him to the cockroach-infected theatre and cut eight centimetres off his right leg. Jabbar was eventually referred to an Arabic-speaking Baghdadi doctor who used his surgical saw liberally with poor Jabbar, who was eventually left with no legs to speak of. Thus he was taken from the Royal Hospital in a trolley back to his house.

After half an hour of weeping by his mother, with both arms raised to heaven, it was agreed by all members of the family that nothing was left for the young man to do but to earn his living by begging. 'Yes. You may dislike something but it works for your good, said our Prophet. You see you have no longer any legs. What does that mean? It means you don't have to buy trousers any more. Think how much that will save you.'

Indeed, with just the cost of second-hand trousers, he bought a mat which he spread out in the Saqqa Lane and began his new career of begging, and training his throat for it: 'Small alms save you from big troubles. Give from what the Almighty has given you . . . '

The locals were very considerate. They started calling him 'Jabbar the Lame', although he was actually left with nothing to limp upon. At the opening office hours in Baghdad, his mother put him in an old wooden trolley with three small wheels and pushed it, squeaking all the way, to the place of his work in the more shaded corner of the Saqqa Lane. By the end of the day, he returned home with a handful of coins in his tin. It was sufficient to buy a loaf of bread, a few onions, some dates, a pound of rice and a few other things, just enough for a dinner, not forgetting to keep a few filses for a rainy day when he could not venture into the muddy lane, as his mother advised him.

But human beings are greedy, even in begging. Despite the ample opportunities for alms occasioned by so many disasters, deaths, funerals and burials in this depraved part of the old city, Jabbar the Lame never stopped lamenting. 'Oh, Dr Atkins, God forgive you. If only you left me with one leg, or even half a leg, I could take myself to the Sheikh Omar cemetery and the Khillani Mosque and earn twice as much. Abdul Latif has lost only one arm and yet he earns more than half a dinar a day by begging at the gate of Said Sultan Mosque. He has even managed to marry the one-eyed Fahima and given her father a dowry of ten dinars. No justice in this world!'

The only place he could reach on his three-wheeled trolley was Mulla Abbud Lane, which was mono-polised by another beggar, Hassun the Blind, who lost his right eye in the demonstration against the Anglo-Iraqi Friendship Treaty and his left eye in the war in Kurdistan. On his dishdasha, he always pinned the Rafidain Bravery Medal which he was awarded by the king. This practice brought him in constant conflict with the Military Police who thought that a Rafidain Bravery Medal on the chest of a beggar in the squalid lanes of Bab-al-Sheikh violated the honour and prestige of His Majesty's Armed Forces. He was prosecuted many times for the offence but he managed always to use his blind-ness as an excuse. 'Oh, I didn't see that the medal was on my dishdasha.' The police eventually lost patience with him and seized his medal, whereupon the local people attacked the police. 'Have you no fear of God and Sheikh al-Gailany, seizing from a poor blind man the medal which the king himself gave to him?' The brass medal was restored to its former position on his dishdasha. The loss of his eye was not the only casualty of the war. It had also left deep traces of wounds on the right side of his neck which Hassun did his best to exhibit also to the worshippers by turning his head side ways to the left. This made many people believe that the war had also broken his neck and made his head look like a large water melon which its branch could no longer carry. As Jabbar the Lame wheeled himself every morning to his work, he could not fail to notice the success of his blind colleague. During lunch time, when his business was depressed, he had ample time to think, like all philosophers. Hassun had a strong and sturdy pair of legs, but no eyes. Jabbar had a good pair of eyes but no legs. If the two bodies could somehow join together, they could make one good beggar with the potential to wander and roam in the entire city of Baghdad and knock at the doors of all mosques, cemeteries and hospitals and attend any worthwhile funeral. With a strong leather strap and harness bearing the legend, 'Envy will make you suffer,' the limbless could be hoisted firmly on the back and shoulders of the eyeless. With his good eyes, the top man could direct the bottom man towards the promising places of alms and charities whilst the other could move around freely with his good legs and Hassun on his shoulders.

With this idea in mind, Jabbar sent his old mother to negotiate with Hassun. Both agreed that the country had never witnessed such a clever innovation since the days of the British Mandate when the

'Anglaise' brought electricity to Iraq. With hands on the Holy Qur'an, both men swore to collect and divide the daily earnings equally between them. That is how the first cooperative society was established in Iraq.

The two beggars were then able to venture some ten or twenty kilometres and reach as far as the Abu Hanifa cemetery. Furthermore, there was more dignity in their work. Instead of each begging for himself, each could pretend he was only helping the other. Jabbar the Lame pointed with his finger at

his colleague underneath and shouted, 'Blind and disabled. Please help the blind! Give him some of what Allah has given you.' Just a minute later, shoppers and mourners heard Hassun calling, 'Alms for the heroes! A man who gave his legs for Palestine, fighting the Jews. Help him and God will reward you!'

Thus it was that two disabled men managed, in Baghdad, to help themselves, save, and live comfortably, until a woman, with her feminine wiles, stepped in. Hassun the Blind counted more than a hundred dinars saved under his mattress, a considerable amount of money for a working man in that country. What could he do with this wealth? Another Arab with good eyes would use it for the purchase of a gun. But what could a blind man do with a gun? He could only shoot himself with it. No! The next thing so desired, second only to a gun, was to acquire a woman. 'Oh, don't be silly, Hassun. Bring an accursed woman into our work! No thank you. She will ruin us. You know what women are like nowadays.'

'I know what you mean. But I heard of a woman who hasn't got even half a tongue to say half a word – Fahima the Dumb, the seller of boiled chick-peas outside the Armenian church. What do you think of her?'

He put the question as a friendly gesture for when a Baghdadi sets his eyes on a woman, in halal or haram, no contrary advice can change his mind.

A wedding party was held by the neighbourhood at the cattle market. Hassun was led to her wedding chamber with the traditional chant, 'Well and good you deserve her.' Beggars of all kinds, totally blind, partially blind, one legged, wooden legged, deaf and dumb and a host of others from the large disabled community of the city joined in and enjoyed the roasted mutton and onions prepared for the party. Drunk and merry, they sang and danced and urged the bridegroom to do his best. Some produced borrowed guns and fired bullets into the air. The commotion went on until Hassun came out with the blood-soaked handkerchief to wave and exhibit. He leaned towards his partner and whispered, 'Brother Jabbar, look at it well. I can't see. Is it true virgin blood or is it doctored? The sin will be upon your head.'

The crowd snatched the hanky from his hands and shouted and chanted loudly, 'Pure and virgin by Allah. Well and good you deserve her.' One limped on his crutches, took the hanky and smelt it. 'Yeh by Allah! Pure and clean like the blood of a sparrow.'

As soon as the celebration was ended and the nuptial work was done to the satisfaction of the bride and bridegroom, Fahima addressed herself to the work in hand as a manageress of the cooperative enterprise. The first step she took was to dispose of the need for Jabbar the Lame. If somebody must ride upon her man and drive him by his ears then the woman should be the right one for the task. Therefore, the blind partner apologetically informed his mate that his services were no longer required. Jabbar had no option other than to go back to his straw mat at the Saqqa Lane. It was a very depressing phase of his life as he could no longer enjoy looking at the fashion shops of Rashid Street or the King Ghazi gardens. He thought he should likewise get married to some strong Kurdish woman from the mountains who could carry him on her shoulders and take him begging to the same places. But what woman would take for a husband a man with no legs at all, having to do both the day work and the night work by herself as well?

Hassun was no less depressed by his new position with a dumb woman who could only communicate with the language of her hands to a husband who had no eyes to see what she was saying.

'I can't understand you,' Jabbar told his former mate; 'A million women in Baghdad who do nothing but talk and shout and you go and marry a dumb woman.'

Still on their honeymoon, the bride and bridegroom were left with no option but to re-employ Jabbar, but as an interpreter, translating the hand gestures into an audio language. It was thus that the two men cooperative was expanded into a three-member society.

'What does my beloved one says, Jabbar?'

'She says she wishes that you have your good eyes and could see her beauty and poise.'

Hassun nodded and said to himself, 'Yeah, I bet! If she really has such beauty, the men with good eyes would not have left her to me.'

It didn't take long for Jabbar the Lame to discover that the marriage institution would fare better if ninety-nine per cent of what is said was left unsaid. With that discovery in mind, he didn't bother to translate most of what the couple were saying to each other. The trio lived and worked together happily and successfully. Fahima could play around with her hands as much as she wanted without bothering anybody. With the added member of the cooperative, they could cover thirty or forty kilometres a day and reach almost all the extensive cemeteries surrounding the city, doubling and tripling their income and beating all other beggars in Baghdad. No emblem could serve the young cooperative movement of Iraq better than a picture of this trio, with Hassun pointing at Jabbar, 'Alms for the heroes! The man who gave his legs for Palestine!' and Fahima interpreting that with her hands and her legs to the deaf and dumb. Their sight became familiar throughout the Rashid Street, the Shorja Bazaar, and the Martyrs Iron Bridge.

Alas! 'When things are perfect,' said the Arab poet, 'expect their demise.' Just when the government promulgated a new law organising the cooperative

societies and sent students to study the movement
in Britain, violent demonstrations erupted in Baghdad, prompting the authorities to ban all gatherings
in the streets. The police considered this trio of more
than two people an illegal gathering threatening the
peace and security of the country. An officer stepped
forward and ordered Jabbar the Lame to dismount
from the back of Hassun the Blind and confiscated
the leather harness. Being dumb, Fahima was help-
less and could not help her husband by resorting to
the traditional protest of wailing and swearing
at the police. Instead, Maitre Hasan Abu Adas,
advocate, applied to court to restore the human right
of the two disabled gentlemen to ride on each other.
Being deficient in faculties, he argued, they were
only endeavouring to make one complete human
being out of the two half bodies, one without legs
and the other without eyes.

The judge, however, dismissed the submission and
considered it another futile piece of Arab poetry and
rhetoric. The order was made to remove Jabbar the
Lame from the shoulders of Hassun the Blind within
the next three days and confiscate the leather belt
and harness bearing the legend 'Envy will make you
suffer'. The police, however, were kind to Jabbar
and carried him in their armed vehicle to his former
place on the straw mat at the Saqqa Lane. Hassun
the Blind was taken, with his dumb wife, to his
shaded corner at Mulla Abbud Lane. Jabbar went on

repeating, 'God forgive you, Dr Atkins, for taking my legs from me and leaving me in this state in the hands of this bloody government.'

Without his mate and with the curfew imposed on the city, Hassun the Blind could no longer feed himself as well as his wife. He told her to pack up her things and go back to live with her parents in the Khillani Mosque district. Her father welcomed her back with these words: 'Damn you woman. You don't listen. How many times did we tell you? Beware of the people of the Saqqa Lane. With sight or blind, you can never trust them. But you don't listen. You want a man in bed, come what may! Right! You sit and starve now.'

With the break-up of that trio, the first seed of the cooperative movement in Iraq had sadly perished.

Love per Hour

I knew Sasama, the name I used to give to Salima on
account of her small body, very smooth skin, light
brown eyes, pale complexion and delicate flavour, for
many years since we were both young students at the
Fine Arts Institute in Baghdad. She was studying
music and I was doing painting under the great Faiq
Hasan, father of modern Iraqi art. We were in love,
the kind of juvenile and romantic love you expect
from a young couple in a conservative Islamic country
like Iraq. It came to nothing as I had to leave for
Britain and do a four-year course in art in Camber-
well School of Art and Crafts. Years passed and
Sasama rejoined me in London when I was working
as a freelance translator and journalist.

We started to go out together, long walks along
the Thames and longer nights in my student digs in
Earls Court, both re-discovering our bodies and all
the intricate secrets which God has planted into them
for better or for worse, but all in his mysterious
wisdom, beyond the understanding of man.

'Why did God give us these delicate organs, give
them this lovely rosy colour, decorate them with all

this silk embroidery, dark, ginger or golden, and put in them all this riveting pleasure and then punish us if we touch them or enjoy them?' she used to ask me. 'I think this is really perverse, if there is any such thing as perversion.'

'Ya! Divine perversion.'

Time passed and Sasama started to face her crucial diploma examination at the Royal College of Music. It was late at night when I heard the three short repeated bell rings signifying that it was Sasama at the door. I wasn't expecting her at all that night. Trying to puzzle it out, I went down the four flights of stairs in my pyjamas and let her in. She was wet and tired as she walked under the heavy English rain from Gloucester Road underground station to my Victorian boarding house in Courtfield Gardens.

'What is the matter Sasama? Anything wrong?'

'I want your help.'

'What is it, habibti ? I hope nothing of that sort of thing. We were always careful. Weren't we?'

'No, no. Nothing like that.'

'That is good. '

'They want me to write a long thesis, some twenty thousand bloody words about some musical subject as part of my diploma examination. I chose the subject of the Islamic Sufi chant. I can tackle the subject alright but as you know, my English is no good at all. I am a musician not a writer. You have managed to combine both, writing and painting.'

She gave me one of her enchanting and teasing smiles before putting her arms around me to add, 'And making love, honey.'

We kissed and laughed. I put a one-shilling coin in the old gas meter and lit the small gas ring down on the wooden floor to make her some coffee to warm her up. 'I want your help, Khalid. You are a good writer and you write well in English. Do this for me, habibi. Write me this thesis. They all do that. All foreign students make their boyfriends and girl-friends help them in writing their essays. A girl from Kuwait made her lesbian English lover write a whole PhD thesis for her. And then she paid two thousand pounds to a journalist to edit it out for the tutor. She knew nothing about her subject, "Women's Rights in Islam", but she is now a professor at Kuwait University, surrounded by her gay students. And all thanks to her lesbian English girlfriend.'

It took me some time to find an adequate answer without upsetting her. I used it in washing up the cups and saucers, pouring out the coffee and looking for the sugar and all the necessary and unnecessary little jobs to avoid the subject, at least just for a while. But I had to give her my answer there and then. She didn't come on that terrible cold and rainy night for nothing. 'Salima, my dear,' said I, restoring my friend to her real and formal name, 'You know how things are. You have a generous scholarship from the Iraqi government. I don't have that. I live from my writing and Arabic translation. Writing a thesis is no small matter. Any time I spend in writing your theses is bound to be at the expense of any work other business clients may ask me to do for them. I charge my clients twenty pounds per hour. But for you, dear, I shall charge you ten quid per hour only. Yet, I'll have to double that amount when it comes to dealing with the Sufi poetry. As you know these Sufi mystics speak always in love symbols and erotic mysteries. I don't know how I am going to translate them into these European languages bent on science and rationalism. So, ten pounds per hour and double the fee for Sufi poetry.'

Sasama closed her lovely brown eyes under their long dark lashes and looked quite grim as she was obviously not expecting that kind of answer from her long-time friend and lover. She took the cup of coffee angrily away from her mouth and put it down on the floor beside her. 'So you want to charge me for your time, eh, the time you spend on me! Alright, then. In future, I shall charge you also for the same, the time I spend on you,' she said and looked at me, half menacingly and half sarcastically. 'Alright, I shall charge you for the time I spend in pleasing you. I do have an idea. I heard that hookers in Hyde Park charge two pounds for a quickie behind the trees, ten pounds for doing it in their Paddington rooms and one hundred pounds to spend a night with you at your place, plus dinner and English breakfast.'

She smiled and kicked me hard on my right shin with her high-heeled stilettos. 'Aye, I also heard that they double their charges for any anal use as they find it too painful and damaging to the delicate tissues. I tell you what. You charge me for your work and your time, ten pounds per hour and double for Sufi poetry and I shall charge you the same for mine. Ten pounds per hour with you in bed and double for any oral sex as you may ask me to give you as it is too straining for the muscles of the neck and damaging to the delicate tissues of the mouth and the throat. Agreed, you bastard? We start from tonight. Show me your money,' she said as she started to take off her clothes and show me her wares.

Write a paper and F**k the World

The saying goes among the global community of scholars, scientists and academics, 'Write a paper and see the world.' The implication is that once you write any academic paper on any subject which occurs to you or to your employer, you can always find a venue for it in some international conference or academic meeting, provided that it upsets nobody and that you are a scientist stupid enough to waste your time in writing papers instead of doing something useful, like digging your garden or washing your car. You can then present it to so many other useless venues in so many different places and on so many diverse occasions that no other scholar would notice the repetition. Thus you would be able to enjoy visiting so many places, all in five-star hotels and beautiful locations. They may even pay you generously for your repeated pleasures. You may even win a commission to write another one.

As a casual member of this much respected fraternity, Dr Abbas al-Muhsin happened to notice something else coming out of its activities, which prompted him to modify that epigram to make it read: 'Write a paper and fuck the world!' To the female turbaned academics, doctors and scientists of many Muslim countries, like some of the Gulf emirates, or failed states like Somalia, Pakistan and Afghanistan, an international gathering to discuss the latest developments in breast cancer treatment or the latest archaeological discoveries in Africa, far away from their own home countries, is the only chance for meeting a male partner and slipping into bed with a worthy lover without getting too involved or committed or compromised. The five-star luxury atmosphere and free vintage drinks help in washing everything down. Frustrated lovers, inhibited men and women, disappointed spouses, shy young scientists and all those endowed with the curiosity of science and belief in the experiments of trial and error find excellent opportunities in these seasonal respectable meetings, secure enough from the suspicious eyes of their jealous spouses and watchful kinsmen. Ali Hussein, a short-listed novelist from Iran, managed to explore the pleasures or lack of pleasure of a Sudanese circumcised female historian in a one-night stand during a conference on the poetry of al-Shirazi.

What is more to the point, Dr Abbas al-Muhsin found that the more you fuck ageing females, or, better still, gay male participants, the more invitations and commissions you get. Contemporary

academics have become like the old mariners, with mistresses dotting the world in every centre of learning. In Heidelberg, they may have a blond Germanic female giant for a one-night stand behind the cafeteria; in Venice, a voluptuous, sun-tanned waitress ready to do anything for twenty bucks. In Beirut, a Phoenician goddess; in Tokyo, a well-groomed geisha. What is Soho, Montmartre or al-Ahram Street in comparison to all these great centres of learning, Oxford, Cambridge or Harvard?

Soon after reading his paper, a youngish professor from Bahrain had two great intercourses during the two weekend courses organised by the Gulf Studies Centre in Exeter. It was in that same seminar on peace in the Middle East that Dr Sabiha al-Fadhli lost her virginity to a fair-haired, blue-eyed academic from Sweden, a world authority on Arabic etching.

It was just at that reputable centre of learning, Dr Muhsin met a history professor from Tajikistan, a lovely creature with slit eyes and red cheeks the colour of a Persian pomegranate. She was almost half undressed when she suddenly sobered up and changed her mind. She pulled up her trousers and fastened its zip. 'Oh, no. Not now,' said she to Abbas, 'Not in this conference. We'll do it next time. In the next conference, in Rome. I promise you. Don't worry, Dictoor Moohsan, I need to know you a bit more. I want to learn more of your opinions on Islamophobia.' She got up from bed and fixed her blouse buttons firmly on her buxom chest. 'There will be plenty of time for this in Rome. We'll be spending five nights there.'

As it happened, Dr Muhsin was not invited to the Rome Conference on Christian-Muslim Dialogue and he lost his only chance of exploring the art of love making in Tajikistan.

But the problem of the Middle East has remained and shall remain the most promising field for mating scholars. One wonders how many high-IQ babies it has produced so far. But we can understand why it has remained insoluble despite all these well-publicised and generously funded international conferences, often attended by that famous Catholic convert, Tony Blair. It is just that the participants spend all their time in copulating and thinking of copulating. 'Do you know what I am feeling now?' said an Arab delegate attending an Arab reform forum convened by the State Department in Washington DC whilst ravishing a young American waiter in his hotel room. 'I feel that I am fucking the whole of American imperialism.'

'Yes, sir,' said the young waiter, firmly clutching his one hundred dollar note in his hand. 'But do you know what I feel, sir? I feel the whole case of your Arab Reform is in my arsehole.'

The Love of God and the Love of Man

(Translation from the Kuwaiti women's magazine *Al-Majalis*)

St Ethelburga's is a small Anglican church which
managed to thrust itself into the midst of all these
international banks, multi-national corporations and
giant financial companies of the City of London. At
night the back streets are teaming with hookers and
swaying drunkards, leaving the old Victorian public
houses at Bishopsgate and Liverpool Street.
The house of spirit in the midst of the house of
materialism, the church was bombed by Irish
terrorists by mistake, probably when they were tight
after a couple of hours in one of those worthy
pubs. The IRA apologised for it and paid for its
reconstruction. With their dirty money, it was rebuilt
to become a centre for reconciliation, peace, non-
violence, religious co-existence, inter-faith dialogue
and spiritual meditation. Courses, conferences,
and sessions on faith, meditation, and religions
are constantly held there. The programmes include
concerts, ethnic music of all nations and story-telling

of folklore literature. This is the secret behind my frequent visits to this unusual house of God. Its progressive pastors considered music and singing as a means for dialogue and understanding between communities and feuding nations. There, I heard Sufi and Indian Quali music and Islamic chant. In 2001, there was a session for a story teller from Syria, a hakawati.

The church has also a carpeted and lavishly furnished large tent in its well-tended garden, constructed specifically for spiritual meditation by the Saudi government, of all people. It contains most of the main holy books like the Old and New Testaments, the Qur'an, the Mohabharata, the Rig Veda, the Zoroastrian Zend Avasta, etc. There are also facilities for listening to religious music of most sects and ethnic communities. The church has also an old clock which keeps striking on the hour. I found it abominable to hear it striking at the time when someone was telling a story, giving a sermon, singing or playing music. I was going to mention my objection to the church administration but I was timely reminded that it was, in fact, a good means to keep reminding us – we the lot of greedy and dissatisfied sons of Adam, of old TIME. Son of man, remember: your days are numbered. The clock is ticking away and with it is your time on earth.

I went to St Ethelburga's Anglican church to listen to Turkish, old Ottoman music of Sufi origin.

As I arrived too early for the concert, I went into the tent, sat in a corner and let my thoughts take their course. No sooner did I do that than a couple of young people walked in and sat on the carpeted floor opposite to me. In a few seconds they started to touch each other, embrace and engage in an orgy of passionate kisses. They indeed went into a long loving session. Somehow, I found it objectionable to indulge in such activities in this holy place dedicated to the world of the spirit, religious worship and meditation and not for fornication and erotic exhibitionism. This is really not a love nest by any means. I was on the verge of telling this young couple off and asking them to respect their surroundings, or even going out to speak to the vicar about it, but another thought struck my mind. Their Christian faith tells them that God is love. The preachers tell the congregation, when there is any congregation in the church, from the pulpit that loving one another is part of the true Christianity. This is what is repeated all the time. I worship God in my own Muslim way and these two young people are worshipping Him in their own way. Perhaps, they are only performing what they have been instructed. Oh, God, give us the power to love and not the need to be loved (St Christopher).

Who knows? This is London and not Basra or Saudi Arabia where lovers had to hide away and express their love furtively. An English young man can kiss, hug and love his girl or boy, publicly, in the street or anywhere he likes. But why did these two young lovers come to this religious place of all places to indulge in love? Is it that the spiritual atmosphere of the church moved them into this state of passion, emotion and desire to exchange tokens of affection and intimacy? I have often heard that faith involves mutual affection and desire to belong to one another. It is the love of the Creator in the love of His creatures and the love of His creatures in the love of Him, the Almighty, the loving and compassionate.

But why in front of me? Why should I, myself, encounter this demonstration of romance and dwell on its significance? Shouldn't I have the right to tell off these two young people and ask them to go and have their sexy exhibitionism somewhere else and not in front of those deprived of their passion? I was pondering this question and hesitating when that same church clock struck the hour of seven. Oh, son of man, remember old Time. And it was the time to hear the chorus of the Sufi singers in their long white Jallabias and high brown hats, singing the love of God and the love of man, accompanied by their evocative flutes and their rhythmic large circular dafs. I made my way back to the main body of the church, passing through its rose garden, followed by the two young lovers holding each other's hands and kissing each other all the way to the old and renovated aisle.

Blessed are the Meek and the Innocent – the World in the Ears of a Child

In the impoverished district of Karantina in central Baghdad most families lived in one single room in small and miserable tenements with no bathrooms or kitchens and one single Turkish lavatory serving all tenants, often flooded with dirty brown sewage water. There, within the small confined rooms, they lived, cooked, washed, bathed, slept, made love, produced kids and died. Parents, children and in-laws were thrown together. Young boys and girls in their puberty would hear the exchange of words, the 'Ahs' and 'Ohs' of their parents as they engaged in the acts of the only pleasure they knew in their wretched lives. Sometimes, when there was some light coming through the small windows, they could see the limbs of their mums as they went up and down, accompanied by the Ach and Oy. The younger kids, only half asleep, could hear what sounded to them as mysteries of the language.

Fakhri was dropping asleep during the Arabic

grammar lesson, rubbing his eyes, scratching his head and doing all he could to keep a semblance of being awake and listening to schoolmaster Khair al-Deen giving his Arabic grammar lesson.

'I couldn't sleep for a minute last night. My stepfather was back from the war in Kurdistan. He never gave Mum a minute of rest. Fadhil Abu Hussein, our neighbour in the next room, knocked at the wall and shouted at us, "Oh Sergeant Ismael, please. When are you going to have enough and stop all this? We can't sleep." "Fuck you," shouted back my father, "I do what I like."'

Many amusing situations arose out of that intimate life, confined to a ten by ten room with a battered door and one small window, and furnished with straw mats, worn- out cushions and a primus for cooking, making tea and heating up water. Salima, barely seven years old, was asked by her teacher about the benefit and use of electric light.

'Yes Miss, we suck it.'

'Stupid girl! How do you suck the light?'

'Miss, I heard Dad last night saying to Mum, "Switch off the light and suck it."'

As he was about to go to school, Sadun found that his bicycle was stolen. He reported the loss to the police. They asked him the usual question, did he suspect anybody.

'Yes, I think it was my father.'

'How come?'

'I heard him early in the morning saying to Mum, "Ride on it and push before Sadun wakes up."'

Of course, in this closely knit society, there was a great deal of illicit fornication going on. One child saw his mum bathing herself in a tin tub to wash off the janaba, the sin of the previous night's tumble and hustle. Her son couldn't escape noticing her sagging breasts.

'What are these, Mum?'

'Oh, nothing. Just a couple of balloons,' said the embarrassed woman.

'Our neighbour, Wahida has bigger balloons.'

'How do you know?'

'I saw Dad blowing them for her last week with his mouth.'

Oh, the blessed kids in their innocence!

Through a Hole: A Muslim–Christian Dialogue

Musa Allawi, an Iraqi businessman and a devout Shi'i Muslim, had never missed a single one of his five daily prayers or broken the prescribed fast of any Ramadan day. Indeed, he crippled himself and spent the rest of his life in a wheelchair as a result of colliding with a lorry loaded with holy Zamzam water, on his way to Mecca to perform the third Islamic duty of pilgrimage. One way or another, God seemed to be too busy with other more sinful pilgrims begging for his forgiveness and forgot all about this very devout worshipper. But Musa often puzzled his Muslim friends by his close association with Christian Iraqis. His house in Holland Park was always full of them. 'I owe them my life,' said he in answer to one of his friends, 'That is why I have this soft spot for all Iraqi Christians'

'Come now! What do you mean – you owe them your life?'

Sababigh al-Al District of Baghdad, where he was born, was an ideal place for religious and ethnic

145

tolerance. Muslims of all sects, Christians of all denominations, Jews, Arabs, Kurds and Armenians lived together in perfect harmony. No one heard of any sectarian or ethnic trouble in that area of old Baghdad. There were mosques, Christian churches and synagogues dotting the winding narrow lanes. Shaikhs, mullahs, rabbis and priests passed each other, smiled respectfully and bade each other good day and good evening.

The Allawi family, a very devout Muslim lot, lived next to a Christian family, and the two families became so friendly and close that they often exchanged whatever exotic or unusual food they happened to have prepared, in the typical fashion of the Middle East hospitality, generosity and mutual help. Um Musa (Musa's mum) and Um Josephine (Josephine's mum) were often seen in the street carrying plates full of delicacies to each other. As that custom became very frequent, and probably arousing the suspicions and speculations of the curious neighbours, they had to think of another more convenient and discreet way of conveying the food between the two families. They decided to make a hole in the dividing wall, big enough to allow the dinner plates and saucepans to pass without arousing the curiosity of the neighbours.

'Um Josephine,' Um Musa would call her neighbour through that hole, 'I have just cooked some nice stuffed vine leaves. I am sure Abu Josephine would like to taste them. Here is a plate for you, my dear.'

Um Josephine would rush to take it and thank her for it, only to do the same a few days later with a different dish of Mousilli Kibba, full of lamb, onions and sultanas, all decorated with roasted almonds.

Um Musa had the misfortune of losing three baby sons, which made her so determined to preserve the life of the next baby, whom she decided to call Musa, after the great Biblical prophet, Moses, to ensure the blessings and strong protection of the champion saviour of the Jews. When a violent smallpox epidemic swept the entire Middle East and reached the city of Baghdad in the mid-twenties, she was adamant that she would not allow the authorities to vaccinate her precious son in case that vaccination might lead to his death. But the neighbours' daughter, Josephine, who worked as a nurse in the Central Hospital of al-Majidia, heard that the British authorities in charge of Iraq at that time, knew of the case and decided to send the police with a nurse to search the house and vaccinate the baby by force, if need be. The young Christian nurse hurried home to tell Musa's mum of this imperialist conspiracy. The two families held a council, discussed the situation and decided that the baby should be smuggled through the hole in the wall every morning to Um Josephine to feed him, bathe him and look after him throughout the day and then pass him

147

back, through the hole again, to his Mum and Dad in the evening to spend the night with them.

'Um Musa,' Um Josephine would shout every evening through the same hole in the wall, 'Here is a baby for you, my dear!'

It was thus that the police could not trace the little one when they searched the house more than once, and the baby escaped the hated vaccination of the British rulers of the country. 'With Muslim and Christian solidarity, we defeated British imperialism!' said businessman Musa Allawi, jokingly and added that he probably owed his entire life to the care of that Christian family.

'Not only that,' his friends chipped in sarcastically, 'you spent your childhood as a refugee with a Christian family, and now you are ending it as an Iraqi refugee in a Christian country.'

Furthermore, as he died a few months later in a London hospital, he was actually buried in Christian soil as well and seen off by a large number of his Christian friends.

Service to the Nation

When Abbas al-Kaitani was released from prison after serving a five-year sentence for carrying *Das Kapital* in his waistcoat pocket, a charge which his lawyer tried in vain to prove physically impossible, and another ten years sentence for an attempt to overthrow by force and in cooperation with the imperialist enemy, the progressive, objective and scientific government, he found himself completely unfit for any gainful employment. Having betrayed his party under torture and given the names of his comrades to the nameless secret police, he could no longer go back to the ranks of the revolutionary struggle which had kept him out of mischief for a long time. What could he do? Years of study and learning in dialectical materialism and the social conditions of the English working class in 1844 were of no use to any kebab bar owner at Rashid Street or any import-export agent at the Shurja Bazaar of Baghdad.

The worst of it was, soon after his release, he began to develop bourgeois ideas like getting married, raising a family, buying his own books, sleeping in one room and sitting in another, etc. True, he had always been hungry for the love of a woman, but who would have him? There were only very few female comrades in the revolutionary movement and they had joined the movement exactly in order to escape the marriage slavery. Now that he was out of prison with all that stuff of dialectical materialism behind him, the question of getting married became a matter of some urgency, particularly as he recognised that for a man with his past, he needed the backing of home and family to gain the confidence of God-fearing prospective employers. Yes, he suddenly faced an impossible, vicious circle and it remained intractable. No employment: no wife. No wife: no employment. Even his fair hair and fairly white skin, normally a coveted quality in the Middle East, did not help him in his pursuit. Long hours under the blazing sun darkened his skin and indeed burnt off patches of it here and there on his forehead. But his eyes retained their striking honey colour which contrasted sharply with his eternal navy blue jeans and jumper.

One of the old habits which lingered on with him from the days of the revolutionary struggle was the obsessional reading of newspapers which earned him, among his neighbours, the nickname of 'the politician'. He tried so hard to shake off his old bad habit but he could not, and how lucky that was for him.

One day his eyes were mesmerised by a public notice. As a result of the war with Iran and the rising number of widows, the Government of Iraq had decided to award a thousand dinars, a plot of land and a car to anyone marrying a war widow. Abbas, the politician, did not need any advice or consultations on the matter. He just went on reading the notice, time and time again, like a leaf from the Holy Qur'an until he found himself such a young widow and applied for the grant, the plot of land and the motor vehicle. Overnight, the war gave him most of the essentials he was looking for and liberated him from all his woes. Who says this is a stupid war, he said. This is a war of liberation. True enough, wars are a bad thing and a bourgeois diversion from class struggle, but we have no bourgeoisie here. We have only mobs and robbers.

'My dear Badra,' Abbas said to his new wife after a few months of bliss, 'We are coming to the end of our money. And how are we going to keep our Chevrolet?' He paused to allow his words of doom to take their full effect. 'I am afraid I will have to go out and find a second wife, another war widow.' Poor Badra looked at him with bewilderment! 'Please understand me. It's for everyone. It's for the country, and these unfortunate widows. Someone must marry them, as our wise leader says.' Badra's blank look confused him. 'It's also for the Chevrolet. I mean . . . how else can we keep it going?'

Abbas wedded the fair-haired Aisha, widow of Corporal Ahmad whose Russian MiG 21 fighter-bomber was shot down mistakenly by another Iraqi MiG 21 fighter-bomber behind enemy lines. And it was good. With her he received the plot of land and another Chevrolet, upon which the spouses made solemn prayers for the soul of the late Corporal Ahmad Walid.

'Dear Badra and dear Aisha,' he started one morning, 'We can't keep two Chevrolets on nothing, you know. We must find a third wife as the Holy Qur'an advised and our leader – may God keep him – decreed.' Although Badra and Aisha were quite ignorant of the intricacies of Arabic grammar, they could not fail to notice his use of the first person plural. It dawned on them immediately that they were on the threshold of a new millennium: community life – from each according to her ability, to Abbas according to his needs.

After the fourth wife, Abbas the politician sold all his cars, gathered all the cash and invested the capital in commercial properties. 'After marriages to war widows, there is nothing as remunerative and worthy as investment in real estate,' he advised his friends. 'Read about the landed properties in Engel's *Origin of the Family*.'

But his zealous reading of Marxism left him with wide gaps in the Islamic law of the Shari'a, which is more essential than bread and salt for life in a

Muslim country. He was often seen hitting his head with his palm. There must be a way. The holy Shari'a Law is capable of anything. How did the Khalifs keep more than a thousand women each? How did they overcome the restriction to four wives only, he kept asking. 'But darling and apple of my eye, they were Khalifs. You are not a Khalif, are you?' one of his wives said. Abbas would then sit in despair leafing aimlessly through the heavy volumes of Shari'a books in front of him. 'Oh, it's so unfair. No bloody room for honest enterprise. I could become the richest man in Iraq, I could.'

'God is merciful!' his four wives would say to him. And so He was. Another public announcement brought him the happy news that the government, in deference to the nationalist cohesion of the country and the safeguarding of the people's security and interests, decided to reward every man who got rid of his foreign wife with a grant of two thousand dinars, a plot of land and a car. 'God is merciful and all compassionate.'

Abbas went straightaway to the Nationality Department and took photostat copies of all documents relating to his wives. Not only did he prove that Badra was of foreign extraction but, in fact, of Iranian origin as well. She was simply an enemy subject, and for that he received an extra allowance of another thousand dinars for ridding the homeland of a potential Mata Hari. He divided everything equally between himself and Badra: two-thirds for him and one-third for her!

With the new riches and successes heaped on Abbas, his eyes were turned to greener pastures. No longer was he interested in any simple widow in black with nothing to bless herself with other than a dead soldier's pension. Now his attention lurked behind the wealthier widows of high-ranking officers with palaces in the luxurious suburbs of Baghdad and Mosul, and maybe with a few hundred acres of agricultural land complete with cows, horses, water pump and Chevrolet. Like a rich merchant and a prospective buyer viewing a new property or a new consignment of merchandise, Abbas al-Kaitani went from town to town viewing the various funerals of war heroes and martyrs, with sorrowful eyes, downcast head and a busy mind evaluating the movables and immovables within his sight.

Soon after the completion of one such transaction with the widow of an artillery captain from Basrah and the embarkation of divorce proceedings of his third foreign wife, he was startled by an unexpected caller who came with baggage in one hand and military identity card in another demanding his wife's 'award'. 'I am Aisha's late husband, Corporal Ahmad Walid of Squadron 3 Southern Bomber Command'.

'You are dead. Do you want to see your death certificate?'

'I was taken prisoner. I escaped. I demand my due.'

'Alright, you can have your wife back if you want.'

'That is a fine thing to say. A man gives his life for his country and gets nothing for it other than his old woman. All the time he is dead another man sleeps with her and recoups his reward! Is this justice?'

'But you have not lost your life, praise be to Allah. You have come back.'

'Be careful,' said Ahmad, 'Be careful. Don't raise your voice! Someone from the Intelligence Department may hear you and take back the grant – car and all. We'll both lose, won't we?'

Abbas saw the point immediately and with the shrewd mind of a businessman preferred discretion to argument. Best thing that they discussed the matter inside, over a bottle of beer.

'Alright, you take Aisha back, and I keep the money.'

'No thank you,' said dead Corporal Ahmad Walid, 'Best thing is to look at it this way. As far as the world is concerned I am dead and buried and you are married to my Aisha. You have my Death Certificate and you also have her Marriage Contract. Nothing else matters. You have both papers in your hand and this is a paper country, or is it not?'

Abbas was very impressed by this unusual power of logic and reasoning and could not conceal his admiration.

'Tell me, my friend, how many years did you spend in prison, and where was that?'

'Nugrat al-Salman concentration camp. Five years.'

'I was there myself, my dear fellow. Block B2.'

'Oh, posh! *Das Kapital and the Principles of Socialist Economy*. I was only in Block C4, Socialism: Utopian and Scientific. Remember Comrade Abbas the Talky Walky?'

'"Abbas the Talky Walky"?! That was me!'

'Don't say!'

'You are not by any chance the same Ahmad Che Guevara?'

'The very same. Aye! Che Guevara!'

'My dear fellow,' said Abbas and rushed to embrace his former comrade and kiss him on both cheeks like one who had come from the world of the dead.

As two ex-comrades with so much in common, including one wife, they shared a second bottle of beer, over which Abbas made a worthwhile proposition.

'Listen, Che Guevara, why not join me in this business?'

'What business?'

'The business of marrying war widows in time of abundance in the spring and divorcing them in time of scarcity in the winter.'

'When both sides get bogged down by rain and mud.'

'That is right.'

'Tell me more about it. This sounds like a reasonable line of business. But please take no notice of what I said about Aisha. After all, what is a wife between friends?'

And more did Abbas tell him. He did not need to sleep with all of them. He did not need to sleep with them at all.

'It's so simple,' said Abbas, 'You needn't worry about their appearance or how they smell in bed.'

Ahmad was willing to take up any freelance work which kept him away from the war and Abbas's promising proposal sounded like a nightingale serenade to his ears. All that was needed was a new identity card which was easily obtained for him on the black market. He was then accommodated in one of Abbas's many properties and with a war widow to match, carefully selected with a dubious origin with a view to the divorce allowance. The two men were frequently seen driving their identical Chevrolets from one military funeral to another. It was a partnership which warranted the highest award in business management and capital accumulation. Abbas al-Kaitani became a trade name and a man feared as much as loved. He became the wealthiest war widows' husband in the whole of the Babylon province. Even the Military Recruiting Office could not touch him. When Ahmad was called for military service, Abbas took Fatima, Basima, Halima and Hakima, to the Military Recruitment Office and caused an uproar.

'Have you no fear of God? How could you?' he

defied the Recruiting Major. 'How could you ever think of it? Do you really want these four poor widows to be re-widowed all over again? Have you no regard at all for public funds and the Treasury? I am not going to stay in this accursed town any longer.'

He did not wait for an answer. He just took Ahmad by the arm and stormed out of the office followed by Ahmad's four wives, in their order of seniority.

'We are moving north to Kurdistan,' he told Ahmad on the way home. 'There is too much competition here.' It was indeed true. Even Aliya, the baker, stopped making bread and set up her own match-making agency arranging marriages with war widows at exorbitant fees. Rumours even went around that some of her clients were not genuine war widows at all, and the wretched husbands had to pay back the allowances and end up with wives to contend with. Other rumours insisted that, in collusion with someone in the Births and Deaths Department, she was obtaining fake death certificates as many other people were doing. How else could one explain the inexplicable discrepancies between the benign figures of the number of men killed in battle according to the military communiqués and the eventual number of war widows applying for re-marriage allowances?

Furthermore, Abbas's empire was now threatened by the reported intention of Aliya, the baker-match-maker, to marry Hamza, the monumental stonemason who had quietly, and completely unnoticed by anyone, carved for himself a spacious niche in the wealth of the nation by carving up the names and ranks of dead soldiers on their gravestones.

With his considerable influence and underhand access to government confidential papers, Abbas received a note that the Leader was about to issue a new decree for the Arabisation of Kurdistan, offering every bona-fide citizen of proven Arab blood five thousand dinars, plus a plot of land, a car and a new colour television set for moving home and settling in the Kurdish region of Iraq. 'There is going to be real gold in Kurdistan soon,' he told Ahmad and pressed his foot down on the accelerator.

He converted all their properties in Babylon to cash and rumbled on in a convoy of four dusty vans to Kirkuk. 'Between the ten of us, we'll have ten television sets. All we have to do is to split up for a few weeks and apply separately.'

Abbas spent almost the whole journey to Kirkuk, some fourteen hours of constant driving, on barren lands abandoned by the cultivators, explaining the principles of mobility, recalling how the French commune became an easy target for the forces of the bourgeoisie to destroy, because of its immobility. That was also the effect of European feudalism. If only the barons had converted their serfs into gold by selling them off as slaves to the Khalifs, Europe would still be governed by the Holy Roman Emperor and the Muslim rulers would have had no need to enslave their own people. Thus, Abbas decided this time to put all the capital of the partnership into bonds and foreign currency. All the assets of the world, both public and private, he argued, would be eventually but inevitably reduced to two items: the dollar and the rouble. The struggle between the two bank notes would decide the outcome of the class struggle and the future of human civilisation. Three months later, the native currency of Iraq collapsed under the weight of the imported tanks and armour. A rumour went around in London that the Military Attaché's office of the Iraqi Embassy had failed to pay the bill of the London clinic for the treatment of a lieutenant general's wife for obesity. The story was, in fact, quite innocent and had nothing to do with any lack of funds. The officer in charge at the office, a most amiable and congenial young man with a charming little moustache, had only thrown the bill into the wastepaper basket on the mistaken assumption that it was another bill from his gambling casino. But the brief lives given to the story in the *Financial Times* started a run on the dinar and Abbas's partnership's capital of foreign currency portfolio doubled its value overnight.

'Our next marriage will have to be awarded in convertible dollars. I won't accept their rotten dinars,' Abbas remarked. 'And mind you, Ahmad, next time you decide on a certain war widow, make sure that her husband has really died. Ask her to take you to his grave and dig him up if needs be. We can't afford to make the same mistake as last month and lose our allowance.'

'You know,' said Ahmad after a while, 'what is really wrong with this country is that merit and enterprise are never rewarded. In any other place the highest honours would have been showered on you by now. But not here! Here they give their medals to people who compile names of camels and transplant the testicles of a rabbit.

'To hell with their medals,' replied Abbas, 'Unconvertible trash!'

But Ahmad was wrong in his judgement. Abbas's acumen could not be ignored forever, particularly as he projected himself as a notable philanthropist and patriot donating generously to this and that war victims' fund. The authorities found his talent in mixing Marxist logic with old Arabic rhetoric so convincing that all the provincial governors of the country started to hire him to write for them their speeches to the recruitment meetings, arguing the case of the wars of liberation and their justice and justifiability.

'Oh, we have no quarrel with a communist like Comrade Abbas al-Kaitani,' said the Governor of Nineveh. 'In him you have a decent citizen, faithful to his country – a true patriot. If all communists were like him we would put them in our heart of hearts.' These sentiments reached the highest echelons of office but the ubiquitous Leader, who was always the first to know of anything happening in the country, was again the only one who had fully understood what was behind Abbas's work. It was, therefore, not very long before the entire population of Babylon read or, as in most cases, had someone read for them a republican decree splashed all over the national newspapers that the Leader had decided in his infinite wisdom to decorate Abbas al-Kaitani with the Rafidain Medal Grade 1 for his valuable service to the nation.

What did Adam say to Eve?

I have often wondered, what did Adam say to Eve when he first saw her in paradise? I thought, most probably he asked her the same question which is in the mind of all Muslims: 'Are you virgin or not?'

My question, however, aroused the interest of my friends at the café in Whitley's. I wish that some of my readers join in this discussion which followed.

Dr Hasan Majid said, 'I think that Adam's first words came in the form of a different question. He asked her, "Do you love me?"

'"You know I do. There is no one else around here except the angels and they are of no use to me."'

My friend Abu Yasin intervened here and made this comment. 'No. I don't think it was him who first started the conversation. It is always women who open their mouths first. It must have been Eve who spoke first. She asked him, "Do you have a condom with you?" On hearing that he had never heard of it before, she cursed and said painfully, "Oh, the poor world!" Nine months later, she gave birth to twins, two delinquent brothers. As soon as they grew up, they fought each other over a woman and one of

163

them killed the other and with that the history of man began.'

Professor Omar al-Muhsin, an eminent scholar in Arabic studies, was with us also. Like all scholars of Arabic, he contradicted all that had been said by the others. 'No! Not at all. You are all wrong. What happened was like this. Eve started by addressing herself to Adam, saying, "Oh Adam. Ya abu al-Basharia . . . " She was interrupted immediately. "Oh woman, watch your grammar, you stupid woman! Ya aba al basharia, not abu al-Basharia. Remember the Nida article."'

The notable Iraqi sociologist, Dr Hussien Sa'id, returned to what he had heard from Abu Yasin and added this contribution to this very important subject. He expressed the view that, 'Our mother, Eve, was not like our latter-day females who don't hesitate to ask a friend who gives them a lift, "By the way, do you have a condom with you?" No, Eve wouldn't ask such a question. In my opinion, it was Adam who asked her, "Are you on the pill?" Whereupon she replied, like all crafty calculating girls, "Yes, to be sure." She really was worried that he might soon abandon her, a mere brown woman, and fall for one of those lovely blond hurias, roaming around in Paradise looking desperately for a lover to take their virginity. It was thus that Eve cheated her man and filled the world with her offspring as we know now.'

As we went on with this important discussion, an Arab businessman from the Gulf joined us. He made a fortune from laundering all the millions of dollars stolen from the Iraqi treasury. I don't recall his exact name for he had managed to launder his own name as well as the names of the scores of other Middle East businessmen and high-ranking bureaucrats. Without any invitation, he interrupted everybody and asked, 'Brothers, what are you discussing? Anything about the price of gold?'

'No. We were considering, what did Adam say to Eve when he saw her first in paradise? You seem to know everything. What do you think he said to Mother Eve?'

The man wasted no time, as we had done, in providing us with his opinion. 'I think that Adam must have asked her immediately and directly, "Who brought you here, woman? Do you have a guarantor? Where are your papers? Are they really good? Why did your guardian leave you naked like this? Come with me. Let me buy you a dishdasha to cover your shame."'

It is certain that clothes were not known there. All Arab historians agree at least on this point. That is why Adam did not refer to her nakedness and say to her, 'Aren't you ashamed to meet a man like this?' He obviously did not ask her, 'Where is your abaya and your niqab and your hijab?' These things came to be used after the fall of man from grace.

'But I think,' said Abu Ali, an old man of eighty-five, 'she must have asked him, "What is this thing dandling between your legs?" She stretched her hand and touched it. "Ohooo! What a thing! Getting big like this! I am so sorry. I didn't know." She went on trying to restore it to its former self. But the more she tried the bigger it got. "Oh. I don't know. How do you get it as it was? Oh frightening . . . frightening . . ."

'She shrieked and ran into the nearest paradise orchard with rivers flowing with milk and honey, followed by Adam with a mighty erection to enact the first act of rape, gone completely unrecorded as usual.'

A Woman in Metamorphosis

With a little bit of string-pulling, Madiha al-Shamy, a young science graduate endowed with a strong sense of curiosity, succeeded in breaking the taboo in her Muslim nation and entered the diplomatic corps of her country, securing a good position in their embassy in London. But no string-pulling whatsoever could help her in travelling by herself without a husband or a mahram, that is, a male chaperon. Unable to find a suitable mahram, she was forced into a hurried marriage to Faisal Salih, a junior clerk in the Land Registration Office, who had never been outside his country.

As a mere appendage with nothing to do in this cosmopolitan city of London, he could do nothing other than while away the time by drifting from one café to another within the Arab-land of London, stretching from Edgware Road to Queensway and Earls Court. There, he met many of his compatriots in a likewise life of idleness: refugees, asylum seekers, failed students, drug dealers and high-class pimps. They sat and discussed ad infinitum their two branches of knowledge – sex and politics. On

Thursday evening, a selection of them took the new recruit, Faisal Salih, to Soho to inspect and visit the various nightclubs, striptease cabarets, sleazy pubs and brothels. There, Faisal was infatuated by Suzie, a blonde practitioner from Copenhagen with a pair of long legs and formidable breasts, white like snowballs, and with all the experience of her exotic merchandise, national and international. 'Well, to say the truth,' Faisal Salih said to himself after spending one evening with this thirty-year old Danish *huriya* of paradise, 'making love in our country is really in its infancy.' The casual visit became a regular one, a Thursday late evening ritual, an expensive one as it was.

'Suzie darling, I love you.' Nothing wrong with that loving phrase except that he said it to Madiha, his wife, as she opened the door for him at 2am, totally drunk and delirious. He swayed, staggered and stumbled into bed, took off all his clothes, except his socks and shoes, and lay down naked on his back. 'Darling Suzie, let us do that again!'

'What are you saying?'

'Do it again to me! Thrilling!' said he as he closed his heavy eyelids and started to snore intermittently with his mouth wide open like that of a dying goat.

By that time Madiha was feeling sick with the smell of stale whiskey and garlic. No good having an argument with a snoring man, and, livid with anger as she was, she took her things and went to sleep in

the spare room, spending the night on the sofa, fretting and wondering, 'Who is this Suzie? What was this thrilling thing she was doing for him? Why did he come so tired? Two o'clock – past midnight! What was he doing all this time? Where was he? Why is he asking me for more money all the time? "Thrilling!" What were they doing? They do strange things here in the West.'

Dawn broke at last with Madiha still awake, wondering and waiting impatiently for the stressful interrogation. She heard him going to the bathroom, banging the doors unintentionally wherever there was a door. 'Come here, Faisal! Where were you last night?'

'With my pals as usual. Why do you ask me?'

'Who is this Suzie?'

'Suzie? Who is she?'

He answered her with the face of an innocent child. Faisal Salih could genuinely not remember anything of his night-time escapade. Certainly nothing of what he had said to his wife. Madiha thought first that he was simply lying and pretending innocence. But the repeated experience the following Thursday and other Thursdays made her change her mind. Her husband was not pretending at all. It was alcohol taking command over his mental faculties and cancelling all functions of memory. In vain did she try to stop him from drinking, joining his friends in Queensway and coming home late at night. It was a kind of temporary Alzheimer's. She did think of divorcing him and sending him back to his country and his tedious civil service job. But that would leave her without a 'mahram' to allow her to stay abroad in the lands of the infidels.

'My darling Suzie, I love you!' Madiha became adjusted to this Thursday midnight call. 'Let us do what we did last week. It was fantastic. Where is the whip? Take off everything! Just keep your pants on, yah! with your . . . eh, what're they, yah your stockings! Come on! What are you waiting for, eh?'

The young diplomat followed the instructions. 'Let me see. Why not? I must discover what is going on between these two – this thrilling, fantastic thing which is making him so crazy.'

She took off her nightgown, put on a pair of black stockings, some exotic pants and a bra studded with flickering sequins in green and purple. Having stripped himself naked, and with his strong peasant arms, he lifted her over his head and threw her onto the bed landing on top of her. Like a wild animal, he gobbled her boobs, the right one first and then the left, causing her to scream as he bit her. She pushed him away, but he only drifted down, kissing and licking her light brown belly and navel, all the way, further down into her groin crowned with black silky hair. 'Oh, how filthy! How sickly.' No, she couldn't push him away as he barricaded himself with a good grip on both round thighs. Hearing his animal grunts and groans, 'Oh Suzie, Suzie my love,' she yielded and let him be. With that decision, she relaxed and soon began to receive signals of strange sensation and sudden excitement. It didn't take long before she reached the ultimate pleasure. The couple lay side by side, both breathing heavily, but the man soon went to sleep, snoring. A few minutes, and he woke up slightly refreshed and sent his hand over his wife's body, caressing and exploring its smooth mysteries and finally working hard to deliver yet another worthy climax from her. It was something which she must pay for, and indeed she did. He knelt over her heaving bust and thrust his penis into her wide open mouth. Not expecting such a sudden attack or such a use of her oral organ, she choked as he pushed the whole thing down to her throat. She coughed and pushed his head away from her with all her strength, like a woman fighting for her life. But Faisal was not a man to give up easily, certainly not to a woman in this situation. 'It is alright, darling. It won't hurt you.' The attempt was repeated, but this time more successfully and with more pleasurable cooperation.

The session ended with a mighty action which Madiha had never experienced before. Once more, she sank into a mood of thought and wonder. 'So, that is the kind of fun he has with this Soo or Suzo or whatever her name was. But I must say I found his middle finger far more enjoyable then his real thing. Better still is his tongue. Better than the fingers.'

Another sleepless night and more difficult nights and days passed in a slow-moving week. 'I wonder what else he has learnt from these London whores. Wait and see. I should like to know. Oh, what these Europeans get up to! Fancy using our mouths like a cunt. God made our mouth for eating and talking and reciting his holy book and these Europeans are using it for fucking. Isn't that a challenge to the will of the Almighty who allocated each organ for its specific task? Still, I think that making love in our country must be really in its infancy. Oh, he mentioned the whip. Where do they sell such a thing? I don't know anybody who has a horse. Do they sell it in the chemist? They sell condoms there.'

Madiha was right, for on the following Thursday her intoxicated husband involved her in all sorts of wild and not so wild practices, oral, normal, anal, manual, verbal, missionary, sadistic and masochistic. She went along with all that freely, partly out of curiosity and partly because she began to enjoy these secretive acts. Indeed, she discovered in herself a wild disposition which made her look forward to the Thursday orgy. She didn't manage the purchase of a whip, but she went to the off-licence at the end of the road and bought a bottle of Black Label which she hid behind the fridge, only to be taken out for a good sip before the return of her husband past midnight.

It helped her to identify herself entirely with this so-called Suzie. 'Darling, have another sip of this lovely drink from the hands of your Suzie.' She drank with him straight from the bottle. It was no longer a question of one delirious drunkard but rather of two, male and female.

'No. No, habibi. Let your Suzie suck it for you. It's so good. I won't bite it this time.' Yes indeed. Everything felt good, exciting, and wonderful for the young woman. After all, it is European, Western sophistication.

But waking up the following day on Friday morning to go to her office in the embassy and attend to her political work, with a hangover and a splitting headache, was an ordeal. Her jaw muscles and all her bones were crying out with pain throughout the day. But her husband's trouble was far more serious as he found it so difficult to wear his shoes. His left foot was swelling for no apparent reason. Is it too much sex? Too much whisky? Did he catch anything from the women in Soho? He consulted his friends in the King's Head bar – could it be the result of anal sex?

'No, Faisal. No way. I have been doing that to Janet for three years. My foot never swelled. Her arsehole did, though.'

'Go and see the doctor,' added Ahmad al-Basri.

But Faisal Salih had no faith in English doctors. They would only tell him to go to bed and rest.

Time passed and the other foot started to swell. A few days later, this was followed by a feeling of pain just under his right ribs, compounded with nausea and loss of appetite for food as well as for sex. He stopped visiting Suzie's establishment in Dean Street.

'What is the matter with you?' said his wife, 'You can't go on living like that. Go and see someone in Harley Street. The embassy will pay the bill.'

She said and he did. Various tests were made on him as signs of yellow jaundice began to show up in his eyes and forehead.

'I am sorry Mr Salih,' said Mr S. P. D. Tudor Firth, FRCS, DCH, DRCOG, DFFP. 'Not very good news. The reports are saying that you have severe liver cirrhosis. Yet, it could have been worse. This is something common among heavy drinkers. How much alcohol do you take every day?'

Faisal Salih had to say goodbye to his cherished pleasure and bid farewell to the bottle. No more visits to Soho pubs and London nightclubs. He had also to change his pack of friends and find others who felt contented with a simple life and a cup of coffee latte and a visit to the Mosque in Regent's Park. There he bought himself a rosary, headgear of white taqqiya and a new expensive copy of the Holy Qur'an, gilded and bejewelled in China. Under the eminent threat of painful death and ever-present nausea, he had no option but to go through this transformation of his life and his character. It was somewhat easy for him, but not as easy for the wife who had just discovered the summits of the Bohemian fairy mountains. To her, life with Faisal became a bore with no more metamorphoses into wild Suzie. She could no longer find any joy with having normal and respectable sex with her husband, now repentant, restricted and reading the Holy Qur'an every Thursday.

Life became very grim for the young diplomat as she began to lose sleep and feel depressed and nervous. It was her turn to go to the doctor and seek help. 'I'll be alright, doctor, if only I could sleep.' She never became alright, pills or no pills. The next thing she took to was the old bottle of Black Label behind the fridge. The drink made her cry more often and less tolerable, especially whenever her husband tried to be affectionate and loving. 'No, please. No more of that. I don't like it. It is disgusting. How can you? You are one of us, a member of my family. Just like Faris my brother. Oh, no, no. Don't touch me. Look for another woman!'

'As I shall look for another man. He is no bloody good' so much she said to herself with a strong determination and a new spirit. She was shown the way and resolved to continue the pilgrimage.

'Tomorrow, I must take the train to Wimbledon. I discovered where they sell whips. They sell them at the Wimbledon Mews.'